GERTRUDE PITTS

TRAGEDIES OF LIFE

ANNE SCOTT

GEORGE SAMPSON BRITE
CASE 999—A CHRISTMAS STORY

AFRICAN-AMERICAN WOMEN WRITERS, 1910–1940

HENRY LOUIS GATES, JR. *GENERAL EDITOR*

Jennifer Burton *Associate Editor*

GERTRUDE PITTS

TRAGEDIES OF LIFE

ANNE SCOTT

GEORGE SAMPSON BRITE
CASE 999—A CHRISTMAS STORY

Introduction by
MARILYN SANDERS MOBLEY

G.K. HALL & CO.
An Imprint of Simon & Schuster Macmillan
New York

Prentice Hall International
London   Mexico City   New Delhi   Singapore   Sydney   Toronto

G.K. Hall & Co.
An Imprint of Simon & Schuster Macmillan
1633 Broadway
New York, NY 10019

Library of Congress Catalog Card Number: 94-42140

Printed in the United States of America

Printing Number
1 2 3 4 5 6 7 8 9 10

Library of Congress Cataloging-in-Publication Data

Pitts, Gertrude, 1900–
    Tragedies of Life / Gertrude Pitts. George Sampson Brite ; Case 999— a Christmas story / Anne Scott ; introduction by Marilyn Sanders Mobley.
        p.   cm. — (African American women writers, 1910–1940)
    Includes bibliographical references (p.   ).
    ISBN 0-8161-1634-2 (acid-free paper)
    1. American fiction—Afro-American authors. 2. Afro-Americans—Social life and customs—Fiction. 3. Afro-American families—Fiction. 4. American fiction—Women authors. 5. American fiction—20th century. 6. Afro-American youth—Fiction. I. Scott, Anne, 1900– George Sampson Brite. II. Scott, Anne, 1900– Case 999— a Christmas story. III. Title. IV. Series.
PS647.A35P58   1995
813'.520809287'08996073—dc20   94-42140
                                                          CIP

This paper meets the requirements of ANSI/NISO Z39.48.1992 (Permanence of Paper).

CONTENTS

GENERAL EDITORS' PREFACE

The past decade of our literary history might be thought of as the era of African-American women writers. Culminating in the awarding of the Pulitzer Prize to Toni Morrison and Rita Dove and the Nobel Prize for Literature to Toni Morrison in 1993, and characterized by the presence of several writers—Toni Morrison, Alice Walker, Maya Angelou, and the Delany Sisters, among others—on the *New York Times* Best Seller List, the shape of the most recent period in our literary history has been determined in large part by the writings of black women.

This, of course, has not always been the case. African-American women authors have been publishing their thoughts and feelings at least since 1773, when Phillis Wheatley published her book of poems in London, thereby bringing poetry directly to bear upon the philosophical discourse over the African's "place in nature" and his or her place in the great chain of being. The scores of words published by black women in America in the nineteenth century—most of which were published in extremely limited editions and never reprinted—have been republished in new critical editions in the forty-volume *Schomburg Library of Nineteenth-Century Black Women Writers*. The critical response to that series has led to requests from scholars and students alike for a similar series, one geared to the work by black women published between 1910 and the beginning of World War Two.

African-American Women Writers, 1910–1940 is designed to bring back into print many writers who otherwise would be unknown to contemporary readers, and to increase the availability of lesser-known texts by established writers who originally published during this critical period in African-American letters. This series implicitly acts as a chronological sequel to the Schomburg series, which focused on the origins of the black female literary tradition in America.

GENERAL EDITORS' PREFACE

In less than a decade, the study of African-American women's writings has grown from its promising beginnings into a firmly established field in departments of English, American Studies, and African-American Studies. A comparison of the form and function of the original series and this sequel illustrates this dramatic shift. The *Schomburg Library* was published at the cusp of focused academic investigation into the interplay between race and gender. It covered the extensive period from the publication of Phillis Wheatley's *Poems on Various Subjects, Religious and Moral* in 1773 through the "Black Women's Era" of 1890–1910, and was designed to be an inclusive series of the major early texts by black women writers. The Schomburg Library provided a historical backdrop for black women's writings of the 1970s and 1980s, including the works of writers such as Toni Morrison, Alice Walker, Maya Angelou, and Rita Dove.

African-American Women Writers, 1910–1940 continues our effort to provide a new generation of readers access to texts—historical, sociological, and literary—that have been largely "unread" for most of this century. The series bypasses works that are important both to the period and the tradition, but that are readily available, such as Zora Neale Hurston's *Their Eyes Were Watching God*, Jessie Fauset's *Plum Bun* and *There is Confusion*, and Nella Larsen's *Quicksand* and *Passing*. Our goal is to provide access to a wide variety of rare texts. The series includes Fauset's two other novels, *The Chinaberry Tree: A Novel of American Life* and *Comedy: American Style*, and Hurston's short play, *Color Struck*, since these are not yet widely available. It also features works by virtually unknown writers, such as *A Tiny Spark*, Christina Moody's slim volume of poetry self-published in 1910, and *Reminiscences of School Life, and Hints on Teaching*, written by Fanny Jackson Coppin in the last year of her life (1913), a multi-genre work combining an autobiographical sketch and reflections on trips to England and South Africa, complete with pedagogical advice.

Cultural studies' investment in diverse resources allows the historic scope of the *African-American Women Writers* series to be more focused than the *Schomburg Library* series, which covered works written over a 137-year period. With few exceptions, the authors included in the *African-American Women Writers* series wrote their major works between 1910 and 1940. The texts reprinted include all of the works by each particular author that are not otherwise readily obtainable. As a result, two volumes contain works originally published after 1940. The Charlotte Hawkins Brown volume includes her book of etiquette published in 1941, *The Correct Thing To Do—To Say—To Wear*. One of the poetry volumes contains Maggie Pogue Johnson's *Fallen Blossoms*, published in 1951, a compilation of all her previously published and unpublished poems.

Excavational work by scholars during the past decade has been crucial to the development of *African-American Women Writers, 1910–1940*. Germinal bibliographic sources such as Ann Allen Shockley's *Afro-American Women Writers 1746–1933* and Maryemma Graham's *Database of African-American Women Writers* made the initial identification of texts possible. Other works were brought to our attention by scholars who wrote letters sharing their research. Additional texts by selected authors were then added, so that many volumes contain the complete oeuvres of particular writers. Pieces by authors without enough published work to fill an entire volume were grouped with other pieces by genre.

The two types of collections, those organized by author and those organized by genre, bring out different characteristics of black women's writings of the period. The collected works of the literary writers illustrate that many of them were experimenting with a variety of forms. Mercedes Gilbert's volume, for example, contains her 1931 collection, *Selected Gems of Poetry, Comedy, and Drama, Etc.*, as well as her 1938 novel, *Aunt Sara's Wooden God*. Georgia Douglas Johnson's volume contains her plays and short stories in addition to her poetry. Sarah Lee Brown Fleming's volume combines her 1918 novel *Hope's Highway* with her 1920 collection of poetry, *Clouds and Sunshine*.

The generic volumes both bring out the formal and thematic similarities among many of the writings and highlight the striking individuality of particular writers. Most of the plays in the volume of one-acts are social dramas whose tragic endings can be clearly attributed to miscegenation and racism. Within the context of these other plays, Marita Bonner's surrealistic theatrical vision becomes all the more striking.

The volumes of *African-American Women Writers, 1910–1940* contain reproductions of more than one hundred previously published texts, including twenty-nine plays, seventeen poetry collections, twelve novels, six autobiographies, five collections of short biographical sketches, three biographies, three histories of organizations, three black histories, two anthologies, two sociological studies, a diary, and a book of etiquette. Each volume features an introduction written by a contemporary scholar that provides crucial biographical data on each author and the historical and critical context of her work. In some cases, little information on the authors was available outside of the fragments of biographical data contained in the original introduction or in the text itself. In these instances, editors have documented the libraries and research centers where they tried to find information, in the hope that subsequent scholars will continue the necessary search to find the "lost" clues to the women's stories in the rich stores of papers, letters, photographs, and other primary materials scattered throughout the country that have yet to be fully catalogued.

Many of the thrilling moments that occurred during the development of this series were the result of previously fragmented pieces of these women's histories suddenly coming together, such as Adele Alexander's uncovering of an old family photograph, picturing her own aunt with Addie Hunton, the author Alexander was researching. Claudia Tate's examination of Georgia Douglas Johnson's papers in the Moorland-Spingarn Research Center of Howard University resulted in the discovery of a wealth of previously unpublished work.

The slippery quality of race itself emerged during the construction of the series. One of the short novels originally intended for inclusion in the series had to be cut when the family of the author protested that the writer was not of African descent. Another case involved Louise Kennedy's sociological study *The Negro Peasant Turns Inward*. The fact that none of the available biographical material on Kennedy specifically mentioned race, combined with some coded criticism in a review in the *Crisis*, convinced editor Sheila Smith McKoy that Kennedy was probably white.

These women, taken together, begin to chart the true vitality, and complexity, of the literary tradition that African-American women have generated, using a wide variety of forms. They testify to the fact that the monumental works of Hurston, Larsen, and Fauset, for example, emerged out of a larger cultural context; they were not exceptions or aberrations. Indeed, their contributions to American literature and culture, as this series makes clear, were fundamental not only to the shaping of the African-American tradition but to the American tradition as well.

Henry Louis Gates, Jr.
Jennifer Burton

PUBLISHER'S NOTE

In the *African-American Women Writers, 1910–1940* series, G. K. Hall not only is making available previously neglected works that in many cases have been long out of print; we are also, whenever possible, publishing these works in facsimiles reprinted from their original editions including, when available, reproductions of original title pages, copyright pages, and photographs.

When it was not possible for us to reproduce a complete facsimile edition of a particular work (for example, if the original exists only as a handwritten draft or is too fragile to be reproduced), we have attempted to preserve the essence of the original by resetting the work exactly as it originally appeared. Therefore, any typographical errors, strikeouts, or other anomalies reflect our efforts to give the reader a true sense of the original work.

We trust that these facsimile and reprint editions, together with the new introductory essays, will be both useful and historically enlightening to scholars and students alike.

INTRODUCTION

BY MARILYN SANDERS MOBLEY

The relative obscurity of Gertrude Pitts and Anne Scott—the two black women writers whose fiction is presented in this volume, might cause some readers to question the significance of their contribution to the history of African-American literary and cultural production in the United States. Indeed, one of the difficulties of "literary archaeology," the term Toni Morrison, Maryemma Graham, Richard Yarborough, Mae Henderson, and others have used to name the process of recovering and examining previously unknown works of literature, especially those written by black women, is that the dearth of biographical information makes it virtually impossible to make certain kinds of literary assessments.[1] Searches at familiar repositories of information by and about African-American writers revealed very little of the data customarily used to assess the life and work of a writer.[2] We know the year of birth for both authors—1900, according to the Library of Congress—but no information is available as to whether either or both are still living. The only publication information about Gertrude Pitts is that the copyright for *Tragedies of Life* is in her name and that she published the work herself in New Jersey. We know slightly more about Anne Scott. She was born 29 January 1900 in St. Louis, Missouri, and graduated in 1927 from the University of Chicago, where she served on the Fellowship Committee of the National Association of Colleges and was a member of Alpha Kappa Alpha Sorority. Later she returned to St. Louis, where she worked as a teacher. Meador Publishing Company, which published her two books, *George Sampson Brite*

(1939) and *Case 999—A Christmas Story* (1953), changed its name to Forum Publishing and then went out of business in 1966.

Despite the scarcity of biographical information and the lack of critical assessments of any kind, the discovery of these two black women writers by Maryemma Graham and her Project on the History of Black Writing makes it possible for us to fill in other gaps in the story of black literary and cultural production. Perhaps more important, the discovery of these texts invites us to deepen and expand our inquiries into the contours of black women's lives and the black women's literary tradition at the same time that we continue the dialogue initiated by Barbara Smith and challenged by Deborah E. McDowell and Hazel Carby about the existence of such a tradition.[3]

The scarcity of biographical information on Gertrude Pitts and Anne Scott compels us to rely on textual and contextual clues and analysis to assess the literary and cultural significance of their work. Both women were in their late thirties, writing at the end of the period we know as the Harlem Renaissance and toward the end of the Great Depression. The tone and content of literary production by African-American women and men took a decisive turn at the end of the Harlem Renaissance. Although scholars differ in their assessment as to the exact dates of the beginning and end of the Harlem Renaissance, most agree with David Levering Lewis that a combination of factors, including the onset of the Great Depression, contributed to the end of this celebrated period of literary and cultural production. The writing that African Americans produced in the late 1930s and beyond reflects the ways in which black people's lives were affected by the economic, political, and social changes that were sweeping the country. Indeed, black and white writers were influenced by the "Chicago School" of sociology that Bernard Bell describes in *The Afro-American Novel and Its Tradition* as a group of "social scientists who broke new ground in the field of urban sociology and race relations with their pioneer studies on the impact of industrialization, urbanization, and social differentiation."[4] Richard Wright's naturalistic writing is perhaps the most well-known example of this school among black writers. Pitts's and Scott's work falls into this category but its fatalistic tone and attention to the implications of upward mobility is more reminiscent of Ann Petry's appropriation of socioeconomic determinism in *The Street* (1946) than it is of Wright's *Native Son* (1940).[5] In other words, on one hand, like Wright, they represent the lives of black characters who are shaped by the brute force of hostile socioeconomic circumstances. On the other hand, like Petry, they also represent black middle-class life and aspirations juxtaposed against consequences of a blind pursuit of upward mobility without attention to its complex attendant side effects. In fact, Gertrude Pitts's *Tragedies of Life* is a kind of literary forerunner to both *Native Son* and *The Street*.

Yet, until the recent years of scholarly "excavation," of which this series is a part, accounts of the literary production of the period of the 1930s to the early 1950s have included precious few black women's voices aside from the familiar ones of Zora Neale Hurston, Ann Petry, Dorothy West, and Gwendolyn Brooks. In this volume are two of those unheard voices—Gertrude Pitts and Anne Scott—whose writing affords us a glimpse into their particular cultural moment and its issues around the interconnection of race and class, issues that resonate in our own contemporary moment.

The one thread holding all three of these narratives together is that they all deal with the young. While it is difficult to determine whether the intended audience would qualify these texts to be designated solely as children's literature per se, it is clear that both authors were concerned with the raising and teaching of children, the aspirations of the young, and the consequences of choices adults make for the children entrusted to their care. Moreover, both authors depict the effects that the vagaries of poverty, socio-economic change, and racial injustice have on the lives of young people. It is the foregrounding of these concerns that accounts for the moralistic tone of these narratives. Yet to acknowledge this tone is not to slip into a reductive bifurcation of their work into trite poles of politics and art. The narrative strategies and stylistics that these women deploy to tell their stories of social formation and racial identity invite as much attention as the subject matter itself.

At first glance, *Tragedies of Life* by Gertrude Pitts seems to be written as a play. The first page of the book provides a list of characters and the entire text is divided into three acts. Yet the text itself is written in narrative form. Thus, one of the first questions for contemporary readers is one of genre. Written as a cross between a morality play and a novella, this book is situated in the period after the Civil War and the abolition of slavery. The first sentence informs us that the story begins in 1870 on "an old plantation that was still owned and worked by an old slave holder by the name of Charlie Jones."[6] Mr. Charlie owns a log cabin where "one of his old Colored families who could neither read nor write their own names . . . did not know that they had been freed" (*Tragedies*, 5). What follows is a cautionary cross-genre tale, thematically reminiscent of Paul Laurence Dunbar's *Sport of the Gods*, in which the narrator chronicles an African-American family's journey from slavery to freedom and the complex consequences of unfortunate twists of fate, struggle, and sacrifice that complicate upward mobility and bring about its downfall.

Act I of *Tragedies of Life* not only historicizes the narrative by locating a particular African-American family in slavery, but also exposes the power relations that enabled the peculiar institution of slavery to continue long after the Emancipation Proclamation was signed. The fact that Sam and Sue Jones cannot read means that they literally remain enslaved longer than other slaves who were literate. It is only because their children overhear the slave master bragging "I still have them as slaves, they can't read or write and they don't know they have been freed" that the parents even learn they no longer have to live in subservience to Mr. Charlie. Although the frequency with which the adjective "little" appears in this section of the narrative underscores the relative poverty of this African-American family's existence ("little piece of meat," "little log cabin," "little cornmeal," and "little scrap basket"), Pitts represents them as a family whose religious faith, belief in education, and hard work reward them with a better life. Indeed, by the end of the first act, the family is transformed from being "always short of food and money" to "a better and higher position in life" (*Tragedies*, 19, 20). They are able to move "from the little log cabin in the country to the city where the son Sam attended college preparing for his medical course and the daughter Rachel went into training in the hospital for nursing" (*Tragedies*,

21). Indeed, one way of reading this narrative is through the paradigm of the reenactment of the Great Migration, which began around 1915, slowed down during the Depression, and resumed after World War II.

The reader, therefore, not only bears witness to the parents' passage from rags to riches, but also to the children's passage from ignorance to knowledge. Just as the parents work harder and harder to raise their standard of living, the children excel in their studies to the point that they move into professional training. Although Pitts may well have been aware of the gender inequities encoded in the choices Sam and Rachel make, the 1930s was not a period when these choices were openly challenged in real life or called into question in fiction. What she is more concerned with in this text is how social formations and class identity begin to play themselves out as the former slaves watch their children "prepar[e] a different life for their children who will be reared in comfort and wealth in great contrast to that experienced as children in the old log cabin in the country" (*Tragedies*, 22). This concern also raises issues about generational differences and the ways in which they manifested themselves within the ranks of a developing middle-class black population at the end of the 1930s.

Beginning with the end of Act I and the early sections of Act II, the text becomes more explicit with its social commentary. Sam becomes a doctor, opens his office for business, and is "very fortunate (because of his sister's help and experience) to receive many patients shortly after, because of her acquaintance through the hospital work she did . . ."(*Tragedies*, 22). The situation of women of the period is represented by the way in which Rachel gets written in parenthetically in the above passage, and then gets written out of the text entirely. We learn that both Sam and Rachel marry and make new homes for themselves, but after a comment on how modern parents sacrifice, deny themselves luxuries, and lead better lives in the 1900s than did their predecessors in the 1800s, Rachel disappears from the narrative. The rest of the story focuses on Sam's marriage to Corene and the fate of his two children, Robert and Irene. We can only speculate as to why this woman writer told the brother's story and not the sister's. However, in choosing to follow the story of Sam's marriage and his children,

Irene and Robert, Pitts eventually does come around to telling a woman's story by focusing on the relationship between the young, naive Irene, and her older "boyfriend," Jimmie.

Yet, even before the plot develops the relationship between Irene and Jimmie, the narrative articulates the preoccupations the parents have in regard to class and gender. They equate wealth with happiness, and use their money to pay for such conveniences as a nurse to care for their children. They assume that acting "like a lady" will make it possible for Irene to attract the right kind of man (that is, one who will supply all her needs and desires), and they plan to insure their son's success by sending him to "the best college" (*Tragedies*, 25). What readers observe in Act II, therefore, is one of the organizing threads of the novel—a kind of mechanical symmetry to the plot, that moves from the fact that the "young husband wanted a son and the wife said she would like to have a little girl" to the consequences of their attempts to parent their son and daughter to match their dreams for success (*Tragedies*, 23). Indeed, the novel develops through an obvious manipulation of the plot so that it alternates between the life of the son and the life of the daughter. In addition to this apparent balanced attention to the development of the son's character and then the daughter's, the narrative consistently comments on the parents' respective attempts to shape each of their children's lives according to their preconceived plans. The primary consequence of the parents' dreams and plans is, ironically, that they transform the children—"angels at birth"—into greedy, demanding individuals by indulging their every wish and desire (*Tragedies*, 25). The parents are so obsessed with their own aspirations for their children that they never seek to learn their children's aspirations for themselves. Indeed, Irene and Robert's conspicuous consumption not only begins to erode their character, but it also demoralizes their parents and undercuts their aspirations. The narrative traces the progression of Robert from truant to a perpetrator of more serious crimes, and of Irene from a high "society lady-to-be" to a high school dropout (*Tragedies*, 33). In somewhat predictable fashion, Robert falls prey to criminal forces and Irene falls prey to a man who takes advantage of her sexually and convinces her to steal from and even kill her own mother.

It becomes more and more clear near the end of Act II that Gertrude Pitts's narrative intentions go beyond a desire to engage in social critique of materialistic values to a commitment to intervene in her community's attraction to these values on moral and religious grounds. In language that addresses the issue of audience more explicitly, the narrator states: "But girls and boys, remember, that God has His eyes on you all of the time, hears all you say and sees all you do" (*Tragedies*, 42). The final words of Act II are even stronger:

> God's word, 'As you soweth so shall you reap,' is something for everyone of us to think about strongly before doing anything wrong. The ending is always the same for those who do not cherish respectability and a good name. Honor is greater than riches, and if the poor mother had realized this when she planned her children's lives, the ending for all would have been happier. (*Tragedies*, 47)

Moral pieties of this ilk dominate the remainder of the text as the reader bears witness to the death of one character after another and to the intergenerational consequences of wrongdoing.

But it is the melodramatic rendering of Act III that poses the most interesting questions not only about the author's narrative intentions, but also about her narrative strategies. Rather than end the narrative with the death of Irene's boyfriend, Pitts uses Act III to expand the melodrama even further. In other words, in her attempt to illustrate the consequences of immoral behavior, she narrates the story of a totally new character, the nameless woman who had been Jimmie's lover before he became involved with Irene. While this final story remains consistent with the other tales of moral demise, disgrace, and retribution, the reader wonders why so much of this act occurs as a dream sequence. Is it that the author was limited in her ability to bring closure to her story? Is it that she realized after the narrative had achieved its own form of closure that there were additional forms of social and cultural intervention that she had not yet written into the text? Were the dream sequences a matter of a failure of imagination, a desire to inscribe specific religious teachings, or simply a heavy-handed example of narrative framing? Is the tale of the prodigal daughter who has a baby out of wedlock and her forgiving mother a way to reclaim the sanctity of motherhood that the nameless girl's own life seems to destroy? Perhaps the unanswered questions in the plot reveal Pitts's own complicated response to the complex moral dilemmas in which women often found themselves.

Nevertheless, by the end of the narrative, it seems clear that Pitts has an agenda that is not only religious or moral, but that is also feminist in her desire to write a cautionary tale for female readers, especially young ones. The copious quotations from the Bible, therefore, are not only signs of established religious tenets in the black community, but also represent the ways in which the church attempted to police the behavior of women. For example, the narrative ends with a revision of a scripture from Proverbs. In *Tragedies of Life*, the Bible passage "Train up a child in the way he should go and, when he is old, he will not depart from it" becomes "Mothers, train your children while they are young, so that when they grow old, they will not depart from it" (*Tragedies*, 62). While contemporary readers may be tempted to read this revision merely as a form of blaming the mother, it could also be argued that Gertrude Pitts was writing out of a sense of her own historical moment, expectations of women during that period, and the limited options available to them. By the end of her book, Pitts has not only used her intricate plotting and subplotting to reveal the complex implications of upward mobility for black families, but also to intervene in and comment on a social order that had the potential to disempower women and destroy their lives. Ultimately, the plot of her cross-genre cautionary tale about the potential loss of cultural and spiritual moorings that accompanies access to wealth and privilege unravels to reveal its own subtextual concern with gender politics, issues of mothering, and the potential role of the church in policing social behavior. In the tradition of the sacred-secular continuum that characterizes African-American literary and cultural expression, *Tragedies of Life* incorporates the sacred text into a familiar secular context to get the attention of a reading public on the threshold of a major shift in values.

Anne Scott wrote about the African-American community from a different perspective than did Pitts. In Scott's two books, *George*

Sampson Brite, published in 1939, the same year as *Tragedies of Life*, and *Case 999—A Christmas Story*, published in 1953, are stories about families who are less well off financially and socially than those that appear in Pitts's fiction.[7] *George Sampson Brite* is a novella about the antics of a recalcitrant young schoolboy who is being raised in a family headed by his single parent mother and his grandmother.

It is not surprising that Scott begins her book with a disclaimer that "the names of all persons and places are fictitious. The characters are fictitious. The plots are fictitious." The disclaimer's specificity not only calls attention to itself, but suggests that she actually may have drawn heavily on her own life in writing this book. Perhaps she felt the need to protect herself with some sense of anonymity or perhaps she sought to protect the identity of former students and their parents. Indeed, the specificity with which she describes such features as the school, the organization of individual grades and classes, the mechanics of promoting students from grade to grade, and even the curriculum politics in the school district, all reveal more than superficial knowledge about the inner workings of the elementary school system. The text, which consists of nine chapters, is in one sense a collection of interwoven tales whose unifying device is the title character. In another sense, however, it reads as a kind of conduct manual for teachers who had few resources for dealing with unexpected behavior in the classroom.

The first sentence of the book introduces George Sampson Brite as a troublemaker. He is accused by a fellow classmate of "pattin' his feet" during the singing of the song "Th Ole Time Religun" (*George*, 11). Scott not only reveals her familiarity with children's behavior and misbehavior in the classroom, but with various pedagogical options available to teachers for dealing with their misconduct. George's presence in the classroom is consistently portrayed as negative through the language used to describe his behavior. For example, when the teacher disciplines him by requesting that he write his name on the board as punishment for disrupting the class by patting his foot to the music, he "grumbled . . . sulkily . . . shuffled to the board grumbling and muttering to himself" (*George*, 12). The word most often used to represent both his attitude and his behavior is "shuffled." Coded into this word is a class distinction that is also inscribed in the text through George and his family's vernacular speech. In contrast to George's working-class family, Miss Smith, his teacher, is represented as a cultured black woman with strong attitudes about her students' needs. Described as "a tall slender, light brown-skinned young woman with well groomed black hair . . . [who] had no toleration of foolishness" (*George*, 11), Miss Smith has mastered the art of handling students like George. Consequently, the story is structured not only around the tension of George's antics and his classmates' responses to these antics, but also around Miss Smith's responses to him. She alternates between disciplining him and ignoring him.

Another interesting element of Scott's narrative is her representation of George's mother. Early in the text George speaks of her as his ultimate threat against a teacher who does not understand him. Tired of what he believes to be the teacher's unjust treatment, he takes consolation in knowing "his mutha was coming over an' beat that ole hard-boiled teecha up" (*George*, 30). Mrs. Brite, the sole breadwinner in her family, assures her son that she will indeed go "ova there and beat hu head in" (*George*, 21). Through this characterization of George's mother, Scott juxtaposes conflicting class values of these two women. On the one hand is the representation of the teacher as a genteel, cultured, middle-class black woman, who takes seriously her role as the intellectual and moral guide of the young people entrusted to her. On the other hand, there is the representation of George's working-class mother, who, out of devotion to her son, and out of a sense of the class politics at work in his school, is willing to take on the forces that are apparently threatening her child's ability to succeed. As Mrs. Brite discusses her pending trip to the school to confront the teacher, she says to Granny: "She lits thim otha people's chil'rin do as they pleases an' picks on my George Sampson" (*George*, 33). Although the confrontation ends peacefully when Mrs. Brite realizes the school is willing to use physical force against her threat of physical violence, the episode becomes an effective way for Scott to encode her concerns with class distinctions as they show up in the classroom situation. The episode also reveals the ways in which intraracial conflict in the black community got played out in the delicate interactions between home and school and between teacher and student. One humorous episode occurs when George's sister, Lottie, responds to the teacher's absence because of illness by clapping. When her teacher, Miss Wray, returns and questions what kind of creature would respond to someone's illness with such a gesture, Lottie mistakes the word "creature" for "creeper," and precipitates a visit to the school from Granny. Granny's total misunderstanding of the incident and the teacher's remark further illustrate the tensions around class and literary that are foregrounded in this book. The remaining episodes in the book are not particularly striking, except for the ones in which George's constant plotting and scheming threaten his chances of being promoted to the next class.

While *George Sampson Brite* lacks the complexity and intricate plotting characteristic of Gertrude Pitts's writing, it is appealing in its incorporation of black literary allusions such as Paul Laurence Dunbar's "In the Morning," its representation of a black teacher with high expectations of her black students, its inclusion of black vernacular forms such as the dozens (that playful, but aggressive form of derisive verbal banter popular especially among black males), and its periodic references to the larger historical context of the Depression and its effect on the black community. The nine interconnected stories of this novella are told rather straightfor-wardly by a third-person omniscient narrator, who at one point becomes self-conscious about her own words. In describing one of George's schemes to get revenge for another classmate's antics, the narrator says:

> [H]e would snow ball him good and the teacher couldn't say any-thing because the boy would have been home first and that would take the case from under the jurisdiction of the school because according to this interpretation the jurisdiction of the school ended when you reached home. He did not think in terms of the word jurisdiction because that word was not in his vocabulary but that was sum and substance of his thought. (*George*, 60)

The narrator's need to justify her word choice points perhaps to Scott's own occasional difficulty in negotiating the language of her students with that of her own. Moreover, her attention to language and signifying illustrate her desire to inscribe what Geneva Smitherman refers to as the black "modes of discourse" that characterize black oral expression and African-American literature.[8]

Scott's second book, *Case 999—A Christmas Story*, is actually a short story. Although the title page identifies the author as the same writer of *George Sampson Brite*, the copyright page reveals she was also known as AnnaBelle Scott. One of the first distinguishing features of this text is that it takes place in the city, the "side section of the great city," to be exact (*Case 999*, 9). While Scott never bothers to name the city, the generic nature of the story's urban setting, and the opening words of the text that "Christmas was descending rapidly . . . on mansion and hovel alike," suggests her concern with social conditions, especially those of the urban poor. Because she graduated from the University of Chicago, it would not be surprising if this were the city she had in mind. On the first page of the story the reader learns that Christmas was

> descending on the broken down, unsanitary, exorbitant renting tenement that housed eighteen Negro families in a side section of the great city. It was descending down into the damp, dark, musty cellar "apartment" of this tenement where Granny and Sammie lived or rather existed. (*Case 999*, 9)

The social critique inscribed in these opening passages serves as context for the story that is developed in the remaining pages.

The situation that opens the story is Sammie's trouble with juvenile authorities for joining a gang of purse-snatchers. Reverend Jones, "the devoted Negro pastor," and Miss Rose, the social worker assigned to the case, both come to the apartment to discuss with his grandmother Sammie's predicament. What Scott manages to do with this brief story, however, is fairly ambitious, for in just nineteen pages she writes the multiple layers of history and oppression that shape both life and discourse among the black urban poor. We learn that Sammie was orphaned when his mother was killed in a riot and his father died, or possibly was murdered, while in prison. Because of dire poverty and his grandmother's age and illness, Sammie and the old woman are forced to live in sub-standard housing. She is determined to care for him herself and not let him be put in a detention home or herself be placed in an infirmary. The gang refuses to let Sammie separate from them. Like Ann Petry's *The Street,* the text delineates the various socio-economic, racial, and political forces at work to undermine the attempts of this family to alter its plight. By juxtaposing the social worker's case number with the words "Christmas Story," Scott inscribes her cultural critique on the material conditions of the urban poor through irony. Moreover, she bears witness to the his-torical realities of black women's lives when they, like Granny, found themselves in untenable situations. The story explains that Granny had

> lived in back rooms, third stories and basement rooms in the twelve years she and Sammie knocked around together. She had scrubbed office floors at night, taken in washing, worked at odd jobs for a little more than three dollars a week and had done every-thing to keep body and soul together. (*Case 999,* 19)

The issues shaping the discourse of public policy in the 1950s are at the heart of Scott's timely story. Its tragic ending not only reflects Granny's stubborn refusal to allow the State to determine her and her grandson's fate, but it also reflects the limited options available to poor women when they attempted to assert them-selves and take charge of their own lives. Despite the efforts of the social worker, the pastor, juvenile authorities, and the school, nothing was able to save Sammie. Ironically, when the authorities find Sammie and his grandmother at the end of the story, it is clear that just as she saved his life from the riot that killed his mother, she carries him to safety one last time in the sense that his death saves him from being separated from her by being placed in an orphanage.

These three narratives do not in any way paint a rosy picture of life in the period of the 1930s and 1940s. While they reveal the resources, both social and cultural, that the black community had to draw on, they also reveal the tremendous forms of oppression both from within and without that black people had to confront on a daily basis. Moreover, they reveal the narrative desires of two authors to intervene in the material and spiritual conditions that racial and economic oppression created. With varying degrees of narrative complexity and discursive development, the fiction of Gertrude Pitts and Anne Scott invites us to revisit these neglected periods of African-American literary history, and to examine what their texts tell us about their own lives as black women writers, about the lives of the larger black community between the period of the Harlem Renaissance and the end of the Great Depression, and even about our own cultural moment in which we bear witness to how things have and have not changed.

NOTES

[1] For examples of how various writers and critics have used this term, see Toni Morrison, "The Site of Memory," in *Inventing the Truth: The Art and Craft of Memoir,* ed. William Zinsser (Boston: Houghton Mifflin, 1987), 111–12; Maryemma Graham, "The Afro-American Novel Project," *Literary Research* 13 (1988): 27; Richard Yarborough, "The First-Person in Afro-American Fiction," in *Afro-American Literary Study in the 1990s,* ed. Houston Baker and Patricia Redmond (Chicago: University of Chicago Press, 1989), 105; and Mae Gwendolyn Henderson, "Foreword," *Harlem Renaissance and Beyond* (Boston: G. K. Hall, 1990), xi.

[2] Research at the Moorland-Spingarn, the Schomburg Center for Research in Black Culture of the New York Public Library, and other standard resources for doing research on black women writers did not produce much, but conversations with Dorothy Porter, Artie Myers at the Library of Congress, and Tammy Winchester of Information Services at the University of Chicago led to information from less likely sources such as student alumnae records.

[3] Barbara Smith, "Toward a Black Feminist Criticism," *Conditions: Two* 1 (October 1977), reprinted in Elaine Showalter, ed., *The New Feminist Criticism: Essays on Women, Literature, and Theory* (New York: Pantheon, 1985), 168–85; Deborah E. McDowell, "New Directions for Black Feminist Criticism," *Black American Literature Forum* 14 (1980), reprinted in Showalter, *New Feminist Criticism,* 186–99; Hazel Carby, *Reconstructing Womanhood: The Emergence of the Afro-American Woman Novelist* (New York: Oxford University Press), 13–19.

[4]Bernard W. Bell, *The Afro-American Novel and Its Tradition* (Amherst: University of Massachusetts Press, 1987), 151.

[5]Richard Wright, *Native Son* (New York: Harper & Row, 1940) and Ann Petry, *The Street* (New York: Beacon, 1946).

[6]Gertrude Pitts, *Tragedies of Life* (Newark: Gertrude Pitts, 1939), 5; hereafter cited in text as *Tragedies*. Page numbers refer to the reprint of the original that is in this book.

[7]Anne Scott, *George Sampson Brite* (Boston: Meador, 1939), hereafter cited in text as *George*; and *Case 999—A Christmas Story* (Boston: Meador, 1953), hereafter cited in text as *Case 999*. Page citations for *George* refer to the original book's page numbers, a facsimile of which is reproduced in this book. Page citations for *Case 999* refer to the reprint of the original that is in this book.

[8]Geneva Smitherman, *Talkin and Testifyin: The Language of Black America* (Boston: Houghton Mifflin), 101–67. Also see in this book her discussion of the sacred-secular continuum in African-American culture.

Tragedies of Life

Takes place in the United States

— *By* —

GERTRUDE PITTS

Newark, New Jersey

Copyright 1939

[2]

CHARACTERS:

1. Mother and Father ... Aunt Sue, Uncle Sam
2. Son named Sam
3. Daughter named Rachel
4. Mother .... Corene
5. Son .... Robert
6. Daughter .... Irene
7. Jimmie
8. Truant Officer .... Un-named
9. Police Officer .... Un-named
10. Nurse .... Un-named
11. Men of the jury and judge ...... Un-named
12. The Girl [Act III.] ... . Un-named

ACT I.

IN 1870, not many years after freedom had been declared, there was an old plantation that was still owned and worked by an old slave holder by the name of Charlie Jones. On this old plantation he had a little log cabin where there still lived one of his old Colored families who could neither read nor write their own names, and for that reason they still did not know that they had been freed. There were only four in this Colored family and their names were Sam Jones and Sue, one son and one daughter who were very small at that time. They named the boy after his father and the girl was named Rachel. As the children were small they regarded everything their parents told them as being perfectly allright. These children soon reached the age of five and six respectively and the parents felt that they had someone to do the errands to the boss's house and they would not have to go out all of the time themselves.

They had on this plantation a commissary where they would go for their food that they could get to eat which was very little in those days. The most they could get was molasses and cornmeal to make mush and they would have to eat that with molasses. In those days they would always call the Colored people 'ant' and 'uncle' regardles of how old or how young they were. One day 'ant' Sue did not have any molasses or cornmeal for them to eat before going to bed she called to 'uncle' Sam and said ain't no meal and molasses here fur dise chillins to eat. 'Uncle' Sam said "Sue sen dem up to de yard and tell Mr. Charlie to give dim some cornmeal and molasses." 'Ant' Sue called to the children to come here "Sam and Rachel go git me some cornmeal and molasses. I got to work and I can't work on an empty stomach, I ain't had notin to eat since yistidy and got to work in the fild all day hungry". The children ran across the little patch of corn that divided their little cabin from the big boss's home; as they ran away from their little cabin, the mother called to them and said "tell boss to gie you a little piece of meat pleaser." The children went up and called to the boss as he had some very bad dogs in his yard to watch his place and let him know when someone was around at night while he was asleep; so the two children when they got to the gate said "Hello". The answer came back to them "Who is it?" They said, "It is me and Rachel; Ma sent us up here to tell you to send her

cornmeal and molasses to make mush, she is hungry
and she said send her a little piece of meat too please."
Mr. Charlie came out of the house as he had company
from the adjoining plantation. He addressed the children as he came out of the house with the company
walking beside him, "Tell 'Ant' Sue here is cornmeal
and molasses but I cant send her no meat; eat this and
go to the field and go to work". A very little meal and
molasses he sent her; he replied, tell her and Sam to
hurry up and get way from that house. Saying to his
company, "I still have them as slaves, they can't read
or write and they don't know they have been freed;
but the two children heard him as he spoke these words
to his friends; they could not understand but the last
two words he spoke that they had been freed. The
two children were very mindful of what they had heard
because their parents when they tried to talk to them
would always say wait and hear what I got to say before you move. The two children took the molasses
and cornmeal across the little patch to the house and
gave it to their mother and as they handed it to her,
Sam being the older of the two said "Ma, when Mr.
Charlie gave us de molasses and cornmeal he had
another man wit him and when us turn round he sad

dat dey didn't know dey is freed, Ma, what do dat mean?" Freed, the mother could not read and she did not know. She said, "Sam, I don't know what dis is, 'but it is somen dat man is trying to keep out our years, but thank God some day all of us will know what it mean. God is not guiner stand for us to be like this always; but I know what I am guiner do; I don't go now where cause I aint got noth'in to wear, but I thank Sis (Martha) know just what dat is um guine cross de creek to her house and tell her what dat rascal said to my childrens."

The next day 'Ant Sue' took her quilt basket on her arm and a pipe in her pocket; (in those days the old people smoked a pipe) and she went across the creek to Sis Martha's house. She hailed at the gate, "He a dare who live here?" "Me, Sis Sue, come on in here gal where you been so long, I was just thanking about you, sit down on dat chair; what you got in dat basket?" "It's some quilt scraps um trying to make me some kinder o' quilt to cuver up here wid; dese nites is so cold and dem chillins ain't got enought cuver on dat couch where dey sleep. Now Sis Martha, I got somin to tell you what Mr. Charlie sad to my chillins yistidy. I sent dem after some corn meal and molasses

and he had company and de chillin ove head him say
dey is freed, so I come to see if you knew what dat
word means." "Well, weel, sis Sue dat word means
dat you is freed and dont hafter work fur bread and
molasses any longer; you can work and he will hafter
pay you in money for what you do and you can go to
town and buy you and your chillin some cloths, and
shoes to wear and bro Sam can raise his own corn and
hogs and make his own meat; don't you see how we is
gitting along. Now Abraham Lincoln don broke dat
bell and now we is free from old moster and we kin
go for ourself, dat is what is it mean."

Sis Sue speaks, "Listen here sis Martha, is dat
what dat is?" "Yes, dat is just what it means." Sis Sue
said, "Thank God I knew he was guiner pull dise
chains off my feet some day; and it is one more thing
I can tell you there is a little school house up de road
dat my chillins go to and you kin sin your two chillins
over there and they can soon spell their name; they
is old enought to go to school; it is a woman over there
can teach dem everything. She is got a book dat she
calls the blue book elementery and dat book will tell
you anything you wants to know." Sis Sue picked up
her basket and said, "Well done sis Martha, I am guine

home and tell Sam what you said, cause he poor creater don't know he is a free man and um guiner tell him dis very nite." She walked on out the door of Sis Martha's house with her little scrap basket on her arm. As she walked down the little path that led her to cross the creek she was talking to herself; as she walked these were her words, "Thank God, Thank God, I am free at last." The poor old woman went her way across the creek and up the hill to her little log cabin; when she reached the little log cabin, Sam, her husband, was cutting some wood to help keep this little hut warm while they slept during the night, as it had turned bitter and cold. After the children had carried all of the wood and stacked it up in one corner they all sat down by the fire, the little cornmeal and molasses was all but gone and then the poor little family did not have anything they could eat before going to bed.

Then the woman said to Sam, her husband, "I was talking to sis Martha today about what dem chillins told me yistidy and she told me just what it mean. Sam, we is free and don't hafter work for cornmeal and molasses anymoe. We can get some money for our work and buy ourselves and chillin some shoes and closes, the same as her and bro Ben is doing; and then she tole me that dare is a little school house up the road from where she live and we can send our chillin to school and they can learn how to read and write our name. The teacher can tell them everything about us being free. The old man began to think over things with her, finally he said, "Sue, I will git up in the morning and go tell moster that I will got out for myself."

The next morning the old man was up very early (as he usually did arise about the hour of 4:30) and began making his fire to try and warm up his little hut before it was light so when it would be light enough he could go and tell the boss just what he was going to do. As soon as it was daybreak, he looked out of a crack that was between the logs in his little cabin and stood up and stretched and said, "Sue, I am going to the yard and tell mos just what I am going to do because I am free." She said, "Allright Sam and Rachel is now old enought to go to school, they only has to be six years old."

The old man walked out and went across the little patch. When he reached the house where his boss lived, he called at the gate, "Mos Charlie, I came to tell you dis morning dat I am free and I am going to work fro

myself and my Sue and my chillins, so you can gie me
what I want to have." The boss looked at Sam as if
he had been shot and said, "Sam, what is the matter
with you?" Sam replied, "I has been tole that I am
free and I can send my chillins to a little school down
the road and they can read and write our name and I
can get money for my work and buy us some cloths
and shoes and raise me some meat. It has ben 3 months
and I has not hat one bit of meat between my teeth,
and, now I ain't got anything for my wife and chillins to
eat this morning, not one mossel of bread ar one drop
of molasses in my cabin." Then the boss was most
stricken with grief, didn't know who had told Sam
that he was free, then he said, "Uncle, I will give you
food to eat but you are not free." Uncle Sam said,
"You know boss that Abraham Lincoln broke dat bell
many years ago and now it is come to light." Then he
gave the old man a small piece of land to work, and as
he worked he paid him in money a very small salary,
but uncle Sam could go to town and buy just what they
wanted to eat and wear as far as his little money would
go. He worked for one week being paid the sum of 35c,
per day but he struggled and raised himself something
to eat, went hunting and fishing at night hoping to feed

him and his family as he was a very good huntsman and took the remains of his money and bought his family clothes and shoes as they were ragged and bearfooted. After he had done the very best he could with his family, he said, "The chillins has shoes and a few clothes, now we will look for the little school house and send them to school on Monday morning.

When Monday morning came the mother called to her children saying, "Get up chillins we guiner send you to school dis morning." The old people could not speak English because they had never been inside of a school room. The two children arose from their little couch that was sitting beside the wall of the cabin and began putting on their clothes and hard shoes. They did not comb their hair but once every two weeks as they had not been taught any differently; then they ate their little breakfast in a hurry and put them a little molasses and bread in a pail that was hanging up beside the walls of the little cabin and went away to find a little school house that was up the road not many miles away. When they got in sight of the school, they saw the children on the outside playing before the teacher had called them in for their studies. Then Sam said to his sister, "Come, Rachel, we'll go with the other

chillins in school and see what they is doing." When
they went inside the children looked at them as if they
had never seen anyone before. After they were all
seated at their places and began their studies the
teacher said, "Come to me all of you that has not been
here before." The two children, Sam and Rachel, went
to her as she had asked them. They were not afraid
of anyone and were very well trained at home. The
teacher began asking them questions. First, she asked,
"Has you ever ben to school before?" They answered,
"No, we didn't know that there was a school before."
Then she said, "Has you got a book?" They answered,
"No, we never seen a book." The teacher said, "Allright, take your seats." The children went back and
sat down on the bench where they sat when they came
into the room. Then the teacher began having classes
for that period; when she heard all recite their lessons
she called these two children who had never been to
school. The children being mindful would listen carefully to what they had heard until they had already
learned a great deal of what the others had recited as
some of them were having their alphabets. The teacher
already had them write on the little black board and
pointed out to them one letter after the other and told

them what they were; then she said to them, "Do you know either of those letters?" They answered, "Yes, ma;" then she began pointing to them without saying one word; they recited the letters as though they already knew them. Then she said that is well done children. "I will teach you how to spell your name, it spells with three letters, and your name little girl is with six letters." Then she began pointing to the letters. S. A. M. spells Sam. As she pointed to the boy, he exclaimed, "Dat is my name." Then she pointed to Rachel — "R. A. C. H. E. L. spells Rachel." The two children looked at each other as if someone had given them a piece of candy. She sent them to their seats. After a while Sam and Rachel had already learned not to talk out loud in school, so he whispered to Rachel, "We can spell our names and they both laughed inwardly with joy. They thought within themselves that they had almost learned what it meant to be free. Some of the children laughed at them, for their little clothes were not as fine as theirs and of their little shoes being so hard, but their teacher pitied them and would not allow the others to laugh at them or scorn.

Sam and Rachel didn't pay them any mind. When the day was gone and they began to put on their ragged coats and caps, the teacher gave them a note to their mother asking her to go to town and get them a book. When they got to their little cabin, the mother and father saw them, ran to them, hug them up to their bosom and asked "what did dat teacher tell you today?" Sam gave her the note. She said, "I can't read dis I will take it to sis Martha; her chillins know just what it mean," so she went across the creek to sis Martha. "He a dare who lives here." "Come right on in, I know dem chillins went to school terday, because my chillins seed dem, what did dey learn?" "I don't know dat teacher send dis piecer paper an I come to see what she want, I don't mean to be insulted about dim chillins, let me see, come here Jane read dis fur Sis Sue." "Ma, the teacher want them to have some books and the name is on this paper, blue black elementery, number one. You git it up town at Mr. John's store." "Shuh, I no jest where dat us, um guiner send Sam right dare fast till it will make your head swim." Sis Sue went back home across the creak; the next day she send Sam to town for the book. They lived such a long way from town until he had to leave home before day as he did not have any way to ride and they did not want Mas Charlie to know just what they were doing. If they did, he would not want them to send their children to school.

The next morning the children got out and went back to school. The teacher taught them as she did the first day they went. When they went home that day their mother asked, "What did you chillins learn dis dey?" "Ma, we know how to spell your name." Then she added, "Your papa is here wid dat book, was not able to git but one, will git one more next week." People in those days could count very well if they had to make marks and count them. So Sam, the boy, took the book and opened it, when he looked and saw the letters, he remembered just the ones he saw on the black board at the little school house. He said to his mother, "Ma, dis is jest what de teacher learned me today." The old woman felt very good over her two children as they could remember in the book what they had learned on the blackboard at the school house. "Well done, she said, I know my chillins will know jest what all of dis is about. Sam can spell his name and so can Rachel." She was very dutiful about getting her children out to school on time so that they would not be late. A few days later Sam and Rachel had almost read through the little book and every night they would sit down by the fire in their little log cabin and read to their father and mother. They got to be very interested in their book so they began planning to themselves, as they learned the differences between terms in school.

One day as they walked up the road to the little school house, Sam said to Rachel, "We will soon be finished with this little book and when we finish we will have to go somewhere else to school; we can't go to the little school house any longer; we have grown to be large children and our mother and father are very old; so what are we going to be so that we can make a living for them and stop them from work." Then Rachel said, "What do you want to be Sam?" Then he said, "I want to be a doctor." Then she said, "I will be a nurse." By that time the two children did not have any shoes on their little feet; they had walked each day so far to the little school until they had worn the little shoes completely out. Their little feet were bare and clothes were patched but were very clean. This did not lessen their interest in their studies and soon they both graduated from the little country school house a mile down the road.

The parents were very proud of their two little

children and continued to work very hard on the farm, always short of food and money. One day Sam and Rachel called to them and said, "We have finished our studies in the country school house, now we would like to go to the Village school. It is only two miles away. We will finish there and then can go to College in the City. Sam wants to be a doctor and Rachel a nurse."

The father and mother looked at each other in silence; both worried about their financial condition and their children's ambitions.

Nothing more was said and all retired for the night. The children weary from excitement with their plans fell asleep immediately; but those poor parents, lying awake, in their bunk fastened to the wall, talked long into the night about their plans.

The next morning these parents awoke very early, arose, did their daily chores, and called their two sleeping children. They said to them, "Sam and Rachel, come here. We have been talking about your plans all night long. You want to go to the little Village School. You have no shoes nor clothes. The others will be well dressed and may laugh and point a finger of scorn at you because of your torn clothes, and your shabby shoes." They replied, "Never mind that father, and mother, you are doing the best you can for us and we realize that the times are very hard with you and that we are very poor; but mother will fix what we have and we will wear them until we can have better. God will help us if we only trust in Him. We will finish our course and some day we hope to be able to take care of you and mother."

The father happily smiled at his wife with the feeling that his children, Sam at 14 and Rachel 12 were so full of understanding and devotion. They did not complain because of their unfortunate lives but worked harder to help themselves to a better and higher position in life. Then the father through his tears thanked God and placed his trust in Him.

With tears rolling down their cheeks the proud parents prepared their two children for their higher learning in the Village school. The rich and better fed children, neatly dressed (while these poor children arrived at the village school in rags) did start to laugh and point at them as soon as they entered the room. Sam and Rachel, although hurt and embarrassed, ignored them. The teacher at times overlooked them and refused them recitation privileges. In spite of all of these hardships the two children continued; worked hard and accomplished what they planned with honors and made friends of the rich children in the end.

A few years later, these poor parents with skimping and their thrifty living, began to grow a little richer. Their home life and crops improved. Sam and Rachel could now have better clothes, new shoes and some luxuries. No more bare feet or shabby shoes. No more luncheons of cornmeal mush and molasses. No worries about laughter or pointing fingers as they walked down the street or school yard. There were gifts, oranges and apples now at Christmas time. The children now completed their course and the parents were indeed happy.

A year later this proud and happy family moved away from the little log cabin in the country to the city where the son Sam attended college preparing for his medical course and the daughter Rachel went into training in the hospital for nursing. Rachel studied hard and worked hard but in a few years she was earning enough money to help Sam pay some of his tuition fees.

Sam soon had his medical degree and returned to find his mother and father after long years of toiling had grown older in appearance and had no strength to work anymore.

He immediately opened his office for business and was very fortunate (because of his sister's help and experience) to receive many patients shortly after, because of her acquaintance through the hospital work she did, she also made a comfortable income. In the 1800's the earnings were considered large but nothing to be compared with the amounts made in the 1900's. However the home was comfortable for the parents lived happily together with their two children until they married and made new homes for themselves.

After years of bitter struggles and sacrifices and with all fears of lack of food and clothing gone forever, these old parents lived to see their children go through a new era happily married, preparing a different life for their children who will be reared in comfort and wealth in great contrast to that experienced as children in the old log cabin in the country.

(End of First Act.)

ACT II.

NOW in the beginning of the twentieth century, more modern parents sacrifice their lives just the same, only differently in a financial way with greater opportunities for their children. Parents still deny themselves luxuries in order that their children can have more; but what good does it do in this case, in comparison with the old log cabin days of the 1900's.

After Sam, the doctor, was married, he took his wife on their honeymoon. They were rich, came from good families. Upon their return to their new home, they planned their future. They discussed what they were going to do, how many children they wanted to have, etc.

The young husband wanted a son and the wife said she would like to have a little girl. They had planned the names, a boy would be called Robert and if it would be a girl, Irene would be the name for her. Both were very much pleased with the selected names if these children were born. The mother's name was Corene.

A year and one half after they were first happily married, the first child, a son, was born and as planned was named Robert. The father was proud of his first child and happiness reigned supreme in that lovely household. The father hoped the mother's dream could now be fulfilled with a little girl companion for the new baby.

A year later, during the same time the boy was born, a little girl arrived to complete the mother's joy. She was named Irene.

After the birth of the little daughter, Sam, the father, said to his young wife Corene, "We now have just what we wanted in our two children, we must plan their future and see that they want for nothing. We will hire a competent nurse to take good care of them so they will grow up strong and healthy. You know we have plenty of money now and can make them happy."

They hired the nurse and she was very careful with the two children and watched faithfully and closely.

The years passed quickly and the children were old enough now to attend school, so the mother and the father had all clothing prepared for them when the school opened for the new term.

The nurse dressed the children spotlessly and neatly, and then took them to their private school. When the children returned to their homes at the end of the day, and played in the garden with their nurse, the Father called his wife and said, "Corene, tell me what do you want Irene to be when she finishes school?" She replied, "I want her to mingle in the best and highest society. She will learn about and understand the finest people and know how to act like a lady, and be prepared to meet the kind of man that can take care of her, so she will not have to suffer for anything and get all that she needs to make and keep her happy forever. I want my child to want for nothing," she continued.

"Very good, Corene," the husband said, "I want my Robert to be a great lawyer. I will send him through the best college and anything in this world I will do for my son's success."

Angels at birth, Robert and Irene changed with time. Their demands on their parents grew stronger and greater.

When the children returned from school one afternoon, they told their mother and daddy they wanted new pencils and pads.

The nurse whom they hired at the children's birth was instructed the next morning, when she received the money, to go to the store on the way to school with the children and make the purchase requested.

The next morning the children told their mother they wanted clean new dresses and blouses, they didn't like the ones they had. The mother could not understand the children's lack of thanks or appreciation. When the school term ended they began to point out to the mother the new wardrobe they required before they returned to school for the new term. Always telling what the other children in the school had to wear in comparison to their own. They showed their discontent which puzzled the mother who thought the children were getting all their little hearts could want for. They were still so young and difficult and she was not aware of what she was heading for later.

During the second term in school, Irene said, "Mother, I want a new pair of shoes and another new dress, I haven't any clothes that are fit to wear anymore." The son wanted a new suit and sweaters before he could go to school another day.

When the third term arrived they demanded even

more and better things. They complained that the old shoes were too cheap and the other wearing apparel was no good. These darling children were certainly showing their lack of appreciation now.

The mother bewildered by their constant demands, said, "Irene wear that blue silk dress I bought a few weeks ago, you never wear it at all." "No, I don't want to," Irene replied. "Robert will wear his old suits for a short while then if he asks me again for a new suit, Mother will get it later," Corene said.

About a week later, the darling little daughter again said, "Mother these old shoes look awful, this old dress is torn and it doesn't even fit anymore." Poor distracted Mother didn't know what to say or do. She had dreamed and planned years ago to make a real society lady out of her only daughter, who at the age of 11 and Robert, the son, 13 years of age were getting beyond her; She still had her mind made up in spite of all of these demands, just to make what she planned out of these two children of hers. It never occured to her to find out what her children were planning, no one knew but the two children themselves. The following year the children completed school and were ready to enter high school. The parents were very proud of them and felt sure their wishes would surely be fulfilled. They never confided in their children or tried to find out what they wanted to be.

These children never had to eat or carry corn meal mush to school for lunch like their father did when he was a little boy. These children had no poverty; in fact, indulged too much in their prosperous life, had plenty of shoes, clothing, allowance of their own, and always the very best to eat.

Irene entered high school, she asked for a new coat, dress, shoes, sweaters and many luxuries. Then Robert put in his order, and it was just as bad. After attending high school for a month, Robert decided he wanted a new Ford automobile, because he saw another student driving one to school. He also wanted a new type of suit to go with the car. He saw his Daddy that night and said, "Daddy, I want a Ford car; my boy friend has one; they don't cost much."

The following day, without a word to the son, the Father purchased his car and the son drove to school thereafter.

During the second year in high school, the father was sadly disillusioned. He thought his son, Robert, was attending school every day. No, he wasn't, but where could he be going in his car everyday? Can you guess?

A few days later, a truant officer of the school came to the house. He knocked at the door, and the mother responded. "Good morning, Madam; my business brings me here this morning to report that Robert has not attended school for sometime," he said. The indignant Mother replied, "Yes he has, officer." "Why madam he has not been to school now for three weeks," he replied. "Why he leaves home every morning for school," she said. "Well madam; he has not showed up according to my records and my report," he replied with anger. "My son does not lie to me," she replied.

The next door neighbor enters when this man leaves and Corene, Robert's mother, greets her and they sit down to hear the day's gossip. She hears all this woman has to say about other sons and daughters in the neighborhood, and then her neighbor continued, "Corene, I saw your son Robert on the corner with Jimmie and other boys, and they were rolling dice." Corene caught her breath, she felt that she must scream; but controlling herself angrily replied, "You are lieing, my son does not roll dice and I do not believe a word you say." She did not hesitate about gossiping of the neighbor's children, but when she heard about her son, she was very much put out and ready for a quarrel with a good friend. The mother would not even question her son about it.

Just about one month later the police came to her door. The poor woman was in for another shock. The policeman said, "I am very sorry, Madam, but I am compelled to tell you that your son has been placed under arrest." "For what," she shouted. "For that holdup on the corner of Cherry and Broad Streets. Two officers were instantly killed and one was badly wounded when shot through his right side," he replied. "Not my son," she cried. "My son told me when he left the house this morning he was going to school and he never told me a lie."

Later she had the opportunity of seeing her son handcuffed at the wrist attached to another detective. When the poor mother saw this and realized the truth, she fell to the floor unconscious. "Oh, my son," she moaned. Corene, the mother, still could not realize her troubles were just beginning. The worst was yet there ahead of them. The boy had to stand trial; the little Irene had not yet completed her high School course and the family was standing alone in their disgrace. Six months later the case was tried and it was a severe time for this family. The Mother did not think her son's trial was fair and requested a change in procedure. But the judge sentenced her son to die and all of the money she spent did no good at all to change this sad verdict. When the trial was over Corene had practically no money left.

To think of all of the plans and ambitions for her son, ending like this . . . death in the electric chair. After the son was electrocuted the father died from a broken heart caused by this shocking disgrace. The poor distracted mother could not stand the shock and was taken ill when both had gone out of her life. She had only her darling daughter to live and work for.

Things went along quietly for a few months and then the daughter came home from school one day and said, "Mother, I want an evening gown, a pair of silver slippers and a velvet with fur collar wrap. There is going to be a dance held at the "Hot Spot" cabaret. Jimmie and I are going and we know it will last all night." The mother, Corene, hesitated for a moment wondering if her daughter realized what expense would mean to her with the little income she had to manage now that their money was gone. She kept putting off

as a dream what she had heard her daughter just say
The poor distracted mother closed her eyes, wrung
her hands and just wondered what her daughter could
mean. She never realized that she was seeing boys on
her way home from school, let alone talk about dances
at cabarets. Corene in a very weak voice finally said,
"Honey, mother has no money to spare for such frivo-
lities, we barely have enough money to buy the necessary food to eat." Poor weary Corene had lost such
wealth and did not have the strength and courage she
had before the loss of her husband and son. The girl
said to her mother while stamping her feet, "What has
that got to do with me, it's nothing for me to worry
about, they being dead and that we haven't the money
we had before, I want what I want and will get it or
else ... " "Furthermore, you might just as well know
right now, I am not going to school anymore," she continued.

"You wanted brother to be a lawyer and what
happened to him? Then you wanted me to be a society
lady and I haven't even anything decent to wear to a
dance and never look nice anymore like the other girls.
I decided to get a job Monday morning. If necessary
I will take a position as nurse or maid, anything just

so I can sleep in. I won't have to come home anymore; because I am tired; you are a nuisance; I have a boy friend and he can't even come to my house; you are always fussing about something or other; you are nothing but a pest and an old devil to me." The society lady-to-be blurred out.

Poor Corene standing still, her mouth open wide, her arms across her bosom, tears streaming down her cheeks, could not think beyond the training she gave her daughter; she understood that the foundation was all wrong; she catered too much to her two children; she should have never given them everything their hearts had desired and used a different method or discipline when they were young. She thought, is this to be my reward for giving up everything so they would not want for anything. I never believed anyone that spoke against them, never questioned them, and always trusted in them just as I do in God. Now my God, it is too late. My son died because he went astray and now I am about to face the same situation because of my daughter's actions. My dear God, tell me, now, what will the end be for me. Yes, the worst was yet to come.

The following morning, the daughter walked into

her mother's bedroom, and without even asking her
mother how she felt after the previous night's quarrel,
announced that she was leaving. "I don't know where
I am going, but I am going; will get what I want and
show you. You don't have to give me anything more,
I am old enough to get it for myself." She said. The
mother asked, "My child, how and where will you get
the things; you haven't had any training and without
experience you cannot just walk out and collect wages
on any job, because you are determined to do so?"
"What do you care," she replied? The girl left and
slamming the door almost ripping it off the hinges on
which it was supported, ran down the steps to the
street, to meet her friend Jimmie, by previous arrange-
ment, in the store on the corner. He was waiting patiently as planned and could not understand why she
was so late arriving there. The grief stricken mother
came out, partially clothed, to the steps of her front
porch determied to persuade her daughter to return.
She was not in sight by then, and the poor mother
stood alone, wringing her hands and crying, "Where is
my child going and will she ever return to me." She
walked into the house moaning, "High Society, and
here I am all alone again." No one knew what the end

of this would be. Would her daughter really get a job in a position to take care of herself, she wondered.

When Irene saw Jimmie, she linked arms with him, and strolled down the street a little way, without thought of her mother's unhappiness or lonesomeness. They entered a tavern where there were lots of music and many people gathered. She felt gloriously happy here; this was a wonderful experience for a well sheltered girl 14 years old. The young couple sat at a table, in the center of all activity, and ordered their beer. After that they ordered whiskey. The inexperienced girl felt light and gay, then dizzy, then partially intoxicated, and then asked to dance. When she returned to her table, she was left alone while her escort danced with an old acquaintance. A strange man walked up to where she was seated, having observed that Irene was not feeling so well and said, "What are you doing here my lass, this is not the place for you?" She answered rather angrily, "I am here with my boy friend, so what?"

He noticed that she was rouged at the cheek and lip, and her finger nails were painted a crimson red. A cigarette was almost burned out in her hand, this all made her look more than 25 years old instead of her 14 years. He felt that he had better not interfere any longer as Jimmie was returning to the table and might cause some excitement; so he left wondering why parents permit their children to be led into sin so easily.

When Jimmie and Irene left this tavern, it was rather early, so they decided to go to a night club where there was more action. They stayed a while and it got to be late and Irene felt sleepy after all the drinking and unaccustomed heat and stale air in the place.

At home she never stayed up late, so she said to Jimmie, "I am sleepy and ready to go to bed." He said, "We will go to a hotel and spend the night there and then tomorrow morning we can make our plans." Irene frightened, said, "We can't stay in a strange hotel." Jimmie said, "We can register as man and wife, and no one will know the difference." Poor Irene's mother at home worried about her daughter, and the daughter must stay in the hotel or wander around in the street at an early hour, now morning. So she decided to go into the hotel with Jimmie and get some sleep. When they entered his room, they sat around talking things over. Irene, young and very unsophisticated never dreamt that Jimmie, who was very much experienced with women, had been living in this room and his clothing was there. She thought it was a new place to him as it was to her; but she saw his wearing apparel hanging in the closet and she recognized them as the suits worn before when she had seen him in the street. He finally confessed that he had been living in the room for about two or three months, using it as a hide-out; because he wouldn't dare take his things home that were hidden in the closet.

To this poor young girl he said, "If I show you something will you tell?" She said, "No, show it to me." He went to the closet and brought out a large suit-case. The girl asked "Where did you get it?" He replied, "I had it here a long time. Now I am going to show you the contents; but don't you dare tell. If you tell it will be too bad for you." "Open the suit case," she said, never dreaming what was in store for her. She was amazed and was terrified when she was shown too pistols, two machine guns and two black-jacks. The poor child almost fainted. "Oh, she cried, where did you get those awful things?" He started to explain and the girl did not know that she had been tricked from home into this hopeless situation with that type of man. He said, "I am going to tell you

something if you want me to. You will have to do as
I say. I will take you away with me. I am the same
Jimmie that was with your brother the day of the
holdup; but I was luckier than he, I got away. Now
that you can't go back home with your mother, sister,
you had better do as I say. If you squeal on me I know
a good place to get rid of you." He continued, "Now
listen to me. Your mother and father had plenty of
money before your brother got into trouble and your
father died. Your mother spent lots of money attempting to save your brother from the electric chair, and
was still rich. When your father died there was left
your mother enough money for both of you to live on.
You remembered he also carried large insurance policies and left your mother that money. Now she won't
give you what you ask for and cries the blues instead.
You will have to go back home, pretend you came back
to live with her until we get a chance to get all the
money. You know where she hides everything she
owns." Then the girl asked, "Jimmie after I go back,
how do I go about getting the money?" "Listen," he
said, "I will go with you and stay outside of your house
until you talk with her. You tell her that you returned
to live with her and if she will give you a part of the

insurance money left by your father, you will be able to get some of the nice things you wanted. She will be so glad that you returned, she will show you just where the money is, and when she goes to bed, you can signal me by switching the lights on and off in the living room three times. Then I will sneak in without any of the neighbors even seeing me. We will get the money and get away before we are heard."

What a trick to plan against this poor defenseless widow who suffered so much from her misfortune. What a pity and when will the end of her troubles come?

One week later, about six o'clock one evening, Jimmie and Irene left their hotel to go about their plans. They left the city and went to the place where the mother lived, and on the old familiar street Irene walked very quickly so she would not arouse any suspicion among the neighborhood. She did not want the old neighbors to see her back. Jimmie walked on the opposite and the dark side of the street, until Irene reached the house and walked up the front stairs into the house.

No matter how bad a child may be, a mother's love will not allow the mother to forget the child. So,

Irene, with her comtemptible sneaking heart and a
mind poisoned against her mother, knocked very lightly before entering her mother's living room, knowing
that she would be welcome and forgiven. "Who is
there," the mother asked. "It is Irene, I have come
back home to you," she answered. "My God, my child
has come home," the poor mother cried. "Come in my
child," she said while throwing her arms around Irene.
She drew her daughter to her breast, kissed her af-
fectionately and kept muttering "My only child, my
darling."

Mother and daughter sat down in the living room,
and began to talk things over. It got to be quite late
and Irene who was impatient and wanted to get started
with the money suggested it was getting very late and
that mother would probably want to get to bed without
delay and asked, "Mother, if I stay with you will you
give me a portion of the money my father left when he
died?" "Also tell me where it is kept in case anything
happens to you I will know." The Mother was so delighted to have her daughter back again, she said,
"Yes", and continued "All the money is in my room in
the old cedar chest by the side of my bed."

The strain was so great on the poor mother, she

said, "I am going to bed as I am very sleepy," and went to her room. The daughter then retired to her room to prepare for bed. The mother exhausted from doing lots of house cleaning that day and the shock brought about by the daughter's unexpected return, soon fell fast asleep; but Irene scheming in the other room was wide awake. Shortly after the striking of the clock at 1 A.M. Irene got out of bed and crept softly to her mother's bedroom and saw that she was fast asleep. Irene returned to her room and dressed completely with a quick get away, went back to the mother's bedroom and then to the living room, as arranged with Jimmie and switched off and on three times the lights. Jimmie seeing the signal knew that everything was allright and he crossed the street and entered the house very slowly and quietly. He passed the hall entrance and into the living room where Irene opened the door without anyone hearing a sound.

Irene said: "Mother is fast asleep and she always slept very soundly when I was home before." So Jimmie said, "We will go to her room at once. I will carry this sharp hatchet and if she wakes while we are searching the chest you just told me about, you will hit her over the head with it. We will get the money and leave before anyone knows that we are even near the place. When they find her they will think robbers broke into the house and killed her. Remember how cruel she was to you before you left home. Now is your chance to get even with her."

Then Irene and Jimmie went into the room where the mother was sleeping and started to open the chest.

God being so just and merciful had sent a guardian angel to watch over the old lady while her daughter was away from home. She must have touched the poor mother who opened her eyes in time to see that she was going to be slain by her own child. She was fully awake now and looked up at her child with questioning eyes, and saw also to her surprise a man standing at the foot of her bed, and heard him say, "She is now awake, kill her."

Without replying, Irene swiftly struck her mother on the head and she fell back on her pillow unconscious. Irene never waited to see if her mother was dead. The mother did die after suffering for a little while. But girls and boys, remember, that God has His eyes on you all of the time, hears all you say and sees all you do. The day of reckoning would come just as it does for all sinners.

Irene and her lover Jimmie got the little money that her poor mother had saved from the little left her, and made their escape from the house without anyone seeing them; of course, with the exception of God. Irene apparently did not remember God's teachings in the Bible or she would never had done this terrible deed. Irene did not know that the Bible teaches us not to deceive; for God saith, "As a man soweth so shall he reap." Irene and Jimmie bravely went away to another city although the mother had been murdered and left all alone in the world. They thought no one knew where they were and certainly didn't know or suspect them of killing the mother. She forgot that God knew if no one else did.

A few months later when everything seemed to be going along nicely and well with Irene, the murder apparently forgotten, Jimmie, the man who made all plans to kill the mother, the real, truly and best friend to her, began to trouble her mind. Jimmie did not marry her now that she had the money as he told her he would. He had been leaving her alone in the hotel all night quite frequently. He was going out with other women and almost forgot that poor Irene existed.

A few months later Jimmie fell in love with another woman, came home very late one night and told Irene to give him the money she had left from that stolen from her mother. "I have another woman now, I want to marry her as I love her, and don't want you any longer," he said.

"No Jimmie, I love you, I want you for myself; I ruined my life and am miserable because of you and can't go on fighting this battle with my troubled mind alone." The young man still insisted, "Give me the money I don't want you any longer." The poor girl stood trembling before him, wanted to repeat all about the sacrifices she made for him, believing he was in love with her as he said and would marry her when she got the money; but she could not talk or mention her dead mother's name any more. Her heart was broken and tears were streaming down her cheeks. She now realized that she had no one left in the world to call her own or give her the advice she needed. Whom could she turn to in her misery and who could help her now, as she needed someone badly? Where is the companionship she was to get from Jimmie? Father, mother and brother gone, Irene left now in this world without even Jimmie as a friend. Jimmie left the house in a little while, then returned, and looking at Irene with hatred in his cold eyes, and in an angry voice said, "Give me that money or else you will die just like your mother." The girl scared to death as she realized what was going to happen, decided to refuse to give the money and suffer the consequence instead. She said, "Jimmie, I killed my mother for your sake. I left my home for your sake, did everything for you but I will never give my money to you for another woman who is making you make my life miserable." The young man said, "I don't want you and I shall have the money and the woman I want" and without another word he got his pistol out and shot Irene through the heart and the poor girl fell dead instantly on the floor. She received her reward faster than she had figured on it when she killed her mother.

After Jimmie had killed this poor girl, he said to himself, now what shall I do with her body? I know, I will cut it into pieces and put it into a suitcase and take it to the outskirts of the city where there is an old farm house and I can leave it there for a few days. I can sneak back during the late hours of the night and burn the old building with the body in it. He took the girl's body and did just as he was planning to do. After taking the body to this old house, he left it, returned to the city and stayed for a few days. He left home one morning before dawn and set the old house on fire, burned it to the ground before it was light enough for anyone to see him return to the city. When he got back, he took his suitcase which had already been packed for quick leaving, and left his room. He went to a strange city where he felt no person knew him, rented a room at a hotel for himself leaving behind for the time being the woman he claimed he loved and for whom he killed Irene.

Jimmie now exhausted went to bed and fell asleep at once. His mind was so troubled, he was dreaming and awoke with a quick start, and on opening his eyes, saw standing at the foot of his bed, not the woman that had taken Irene's place in his heart but poor Irene just as though she was alive. Jimmie call to her, "Irene" but got no reply.

Jimmie got out of his bed, for the poor dead girl was troubling him, he could not sleep. He dressed and went out into the streets of the strange city and walked all night long. The next day he checked out of his hotel and decided to go to another city thinking he would get away but Irene's spirit still followed him, so he tried another hotel and another city; but when he tried to sleep that same vision came back to haunt him all the time.

He jumped up one night and screamed, "I cannot sleep, Irene just keeps following me all of the time, I must be going mad, what am I going to do? It would be best for me to die." With that he ran around pulling at his hair until he reached the end of the hall on his floor of the hotel, opened the window and jumped from the fifth floor to the sidewalk where his body fell heavily, and crushed his skull. He died instantly with the name "Irene" on his lips. So it ended, just as he tormented Irene, so his life ended, without getting the love of the older woman he wanted as his wife. She had refused to go with him to strange places when he could not promise to make a permanent home for her as he had so little money.

God's word, "As you soweth so shall you reap," is something for everyone of us to think about strongly before doing anything wrong. The ending is always the same for those who do not cherish respectability and a good name. Honor is greater than riches, and if the poor mother had realized this when she planned her children's lives, the ending for all would have been happier.

(End of Second Act.)

ACT III.

IT was the same morning that Jimmie had murdered Irene; waiting patiently for him was his sweetheart; but instead of Jimmie returning, he left the
city without her knowledge. All that day she waited.
She knew what he had gone out to do, as they had
planned it very carefully, but still Jimmie did not return.

She became worried after several days of his dis-
appearance. She couldn't sleep. Jimmie had left her in
a dangerous position—and she knew it. Rising from
the porch of her rooming house, she went into her room
and fell across the bed, crying bitterly. She couldn't
divulge her secret and she had worried herself sick.

No one knew where the young girl was, so the
landlady began to inquire as to the girls whereabouts.
She went up to the girl's room and knocked but only
an ominous silence greeted her. She started to turn
away, but thought better of it and decided to try the
door again. She knocked. Silence! Still not satisfied,
the landlady tried the door. Finding it unlocked, she

slowly opened the door. The girl lay across the bed as though she were asleep. The landlady called the girl's name. Receiving no answer, she hastened to the bedside and caught the girl's hand. She immediately felt that something was wrong. She ran down stairs, grabbed the telephone and hurriedly summoned the doctor. The doctor was there examining the girl within a few minutes. After a short time the doctor announced that there was nothing physically wrong with the girl but that she probably had something on her mind that was worrying her. He asked her about her husband but she only looked at him while big tears rolled down her cheeks. She didn't know if she would even see Jimmie again.

After the doctor had gone the landlady told the girl that the doctor said she was probably in trouble. The landlady asked the girl to confide in her, but she wouldn't utter a sound.

After the landlady left, the girl began to think. She would like to tell the landlady, but it was a secret. She thought, "I haven't any place to go. I will tell the landlady everything tomorrow. I somehow believe that Jimmie will come tonight." She arose from the bed and started to undress, but she had become so weak and worried that she almost fell to the floor. She soon steadied herself and then laboriously proceeded to undress and went to bed. She lay there tossing and turning most of the night, thinking of the trouble she was in. She finally went to sleep as the clock struck three. When she opened her eyes she saw a well dressed man standing at the foot of her bed. She jumped up and said, "Oh Jimmie, I'm so glad you've come;" but when she had fully awakened she realized it had been a dream. She thought to herself, "I know I saw Jimmie; where has he gone?" She waited awhile, but he did not come back. She decided to go to sleep again. About four o'clock he reappeared to her in a dream. He said, "I will not call your name; no one here knows it. I love you dearly, but I must never see you again. You know I have murdered poor Irene. After I left you she haunted me every place I went. I couldn't stand it any longer so I have committed suicide. I am dead to the world. Remember, whatsoever a man soweth so shall he reap." "Oh Jimmie, are you really dead?" "Yes, I will never see you again on this earth." The girl did not know just what to think.

The next morning she felt as though she was in a new world. She wondered if she had really seen Jimmie or if it was just a dream. "He told me that he was

dead. I wonder if the only man I love is really dead."
All day she went as though in a trance. Late that afternoon someone turned on the radio; she heard the announcer say that a strange man had been found dead.
He had jumped from a hotel window and was instantly killed. He was wearing a pale blue pajama suit. In
his room was a heavy blue suit that he had been wearing; in the pocket of his coat was a card bearing the
name Jimmie. When the announcer had finished, the
tears began to roll down her cheeks. She said, "Oh!
my God, that is my Jimmie, what will I do? I know it
is him; those are the clothes he was wearing. Somebody, please help me. I am afraid to go where he is.
If I do, I will have to tell everything I know, and then
they will put me in jail. Just look at me, my condition;
what will I do? Here I am in a strange town; no one
knows me." She sat there thinking far into the night.
It was useless to go to bed, because sleep was impossible. She decided that she would confide everything
to the landlady in the morning. "Jimmie is dead and
I am left in too much trouble. I left my mother and
father who were very nice to me and gave me everything my heart desired. That was enough. I ran away
and broke their hearts. Now someone has broken my

heart. I can't go back home this way. My sister and brothers are living swell and I am out here in a strange land with no one to turn to for sympathy." By this time the dusk was breaking; the morning star had risen. The milk man was on his route, and the girl continued to sit and think her dismal thoughts. As soon as the sun rose she called to her landlady and asked her if she had heard the news flashes over the radio last evening.

The landlady answered in the affirmative. The girl asked her if she recalled the one about the strange man being found dead. The landlady nodded. The girl looked at her as if she was going to scream. The landlady asked her if she had something to tell her. The girl replied: "It is a secret madam, but I just have to tell you." The landlady assured her that she would do all she could to help. This made the girl feel a little better. She began to tell this story. First, she said: "The man you heard them speaking about was Jimmie, my Jimmie. He is the one whom I love and is the one who has me in this condition I am in today. I love him; but I guess . . . . the girl fell unconscious to the floor. The lady got some water and bathed her face. Soon she came to; the landlady gently told her to continue

her story. The girl began once again to tell the landlady all of her secret. "This is the way I came to meet
him. I was taking in a movie one night, as my mother
always permitted me to have my pleasure, but I always
had to be in at eleven o'clock. On this particular night
while on my way to the theatre I met Jimmie standing
on a corner not far from my house. As I was passing
he raised his hat and said, "How do you do, little
lady?" I bowed my head and smiled at him, as I always smiled when anyone spoke to me. He asked me
if he could accompany me to the theatre; I, being
impressed with his handsome appearance and polite
manners, answered: yes, though I was only seventeen
years of age and my mother was very strict with me and
did not want me to keep company with young men.
While we were walking and talking, I happened to
catch Jimmie looking at me intently. When I asked
him why; he replied, "Because I love you." Shocked,
I reminded him that he had never seen me bofore, but
but I said that it must be love at first sight. After
walking a little further, he asked me if he could call
on me. I explained to him that my mother had for-
bidden me to receive company. By that time we were
in sight of the theatre. We stopped on the corner just

in front of the theatre and he outlined a plan by which we could see each other without my parents knowing anything about it. "You will leave home just as if you were going to the movies and I will meet you two blocks away from home." In this way we can go places and do things. I have money and you won't have anything to worry about." I thought it over before I answered him. I told him, yes. We talked awhile and then walked away.

We went to a cabaret party out of town that night and it was twelve o'clock when I got home, one hour later than I had ever stayed out before. My parents being worried had not gone to bed, they called me to their room and asked me where I had been. I told them that I had been to the movies and the picture was much longer than usual. They said that I would have to be punished and confiscated my rights to go out anymore that week. I was wondering how I could see Jimmie, for I had a date with him that Monday. I lay awake a long while that night, figuring a possible way to meet him. I realized now that I loved him also. I decided that I would slip out and meet him in spite of my parents.

The landlady was listening with interest to the

girl's story. She continued: "When Jimmie met me, I told him what had happened; he told me that if I would leave home and come with him, he would take care of me and I wouldn't have to worry. We planned to meet at nine o'clock the next night. I packed all of my clothes and put the suit case as far under the bed as possible, I did not sleep at all that night. The next day I did not go out of the house. Mother, dad and the children went to bed early that night. I waited until I was sure everyone had fallen asleep, then I picked up my bag and slipped out. Jimmie was waiting for me as he had said and we left town and came here. I soon began to wonder where Jimmie got all of his money, because he didn't have a job of any sort, yet he always looked so prosperous. He did not, as you know, live with me but he was providing my room and board. All he asked of me was not to worry, that he would see to it that I would never need or want for anything; then he went away. The next day when he returned I again asked him about the money. This time he told me he had a secret. When I promised not to repeat the secret to a soul he told me that he was having an affair with another woman with whom he was living in the small town where I had come from.

This woman had plenty of money and Jimmie got all he wanted whenever he needed it. He said he didn't love her and when he got all of her money he would marry me. I was glad to hear him say that. Sometime later I wanted a new outfit so that I could attend a dance, I asked Jimmie for the money. He went to this woman whose name was Irene to ask her for the money. Irene said she didn't have the money to give him. After hearing this, Jimmie came to me and told me what she had said and vowed to go back and ask her again, and if she refused he would kill her. Jimmie knew that she had money; he told me that he and Irene had murdered her mother and got all of her dad's insurance. It was quite a sum—and now if she doesn't give it to me, it will be too late. When Jimmie went back to Irene and she refused to give him the money, he took out his revolver and shot her through the heart. Then he took the body and burned it to ashes."

"After he had murdered her, he was afraid to come back to me, so he went to another city. I have not seen or heard from him since. He left me flat, and, now I have no place to go. Now he has committed suicide. Oh, please, tell me what to do. I want you to, please, let me stay here until my baby comes, and then I can go away. Oh God, help me!"

The words that Jimmie had spoken to her in a dream followed her, "You shall reap what you sow." The landlady was still looking at her but had not yet answered her. Finally she asked if she was ever married to Jimmie. The girl answered, "No, madam, I was only his sweetheart, but we were going to get married after he murdered Irene. This upset the landlady very much and she turned very pale after hearing their revelations of murdering one woman just to marry another. When the landlady spoke, she said, "Poor Irene." The girl hung her head in shame. She knew that the landlady did not sympathize with her for such a dirty crime but she was still waiting hopefully for an answer as to whether she could stay there, or not, in her condition.

When the landlady finally answered it was very sad news for the girl. The landlady said: no,she could not remain there; she said: she had a girl only twelve years of age and she did not want anything to happen to her. She said: that this may start her on the road to destruction. After hearing this, the girl almost screamed. When she became calm again, she began to sing an old hymn that her mother used to sing. (I couldn't hear nobody pray.) She began packing up her clothes, although she had no idea where she was going. It would only be a few weeks more now before her baby would be born. The weather had begun to get cold. It was a very disheartened and sad girl who came out of the rooming house, her loved one dead; her guilty secret and her shame failed to permit her to go home and face her people. She walked to an old deserted house on the outskirts of the town where she had been previously. She left her bags in this old house and went to the city, to the police station, to ask for food and some place to stay. They looked at her, realizing her condition asked her where her husband was. She said she had no husband. They gave her an old prison cot and a blanket and she took them to the old deserted house where she had left her bags. She spread her coat and one half of the blanket on the cot to serve as a mattress. She went off into a fitful sleep, tossing and turning all night long. Irene came and stood at the foot of the cot and looked over the poor girl and said, "Be not deceived for God is not mocked. Whatsoever a man soweth, so shall he reap." Irene continued, "I suffered for what I did to my mother, and now you must suffer for what you did to me. God has His eyes on you."

The next morning the girl arose very early and walked out of the house and looked over her surroundings. About eight o'clock she went back to police headquarters and asked for more food. They gave her something to eat but òtherwise no one seemed to pay any attention to her. She ate the little food they gave her and went back to the cottage to think. It was getting cold and she had no means of making a fire. She decided that when her baby was born she would leave it on somebody's doorstep, then she could be herself again without any one being the wiser. Soon pains began to come on the girl, and they kept growing worse and worse. The girl, now not knowing that she was nearing the end, wondered what was wrong with her. About one o'clock her pains were so bad that she could not lie down. About one thirty the little child was born with no one there to help the poor girl. She started to pray, "Oh God, help me, what am I to do?" The Lord heard the girl's prayer and sent an angel to the girl's mother. The mother got up, dressed and came to the city. On inquiring at the police station about a strange girl, they told her about the girl in the dilapidated house on the outskirts of the city. The mother rushed immediately out to the house. When she pushed the door open, she saw her daughter and the baby lying on the cot. The same angel was watching over the girl. The mother dropped on her knees and began praying to God, thanking Him for everything He had done to enable her to see her daughter again. This mother was a God fearing mother and was only led by the Spirit of God. Something spoke within this mother and told her to take her child home. Her father was waiting very anxiously to see his daughter and welcome her home again. The mother did not try to remove the girl that day, but cleaned them and stayed there all night watching over the two. A real mother will not leave her child; because the Good Book says: "Love hides multitudes of faults." This mother being a real mother with the Love of God in her heart did not have time to stop and think of what her child had done, but was ready and willing to throw her arms around the girl and own her as her child once more.

The next morning this girl was very sick; her mother dressed her and the little baby and started down the street with a prayer in her heart. She prayed to God to give the girl strength so that she might be able to get home safely. The father stood at the window

watching for them to return. Soon he was relieved because he saw them as they turned the corner toward
the house and he uttered a Prayer of Thanksgiving.
The mother immediately put the girl to bed. Her
father asked her who was the father of the baby. The
mother said it is our baby, my child. The father dropped his head, tears streaming down his heavy cheeks.

Two days later the baby passed away. After they
had buried the baby, the girl's father came home and
began talking to his daughter about her troubles. She
looked at her father and said, "Father, I had a good
home, every thing my heart could desire, I ran away
but now I am almost gone; my mother found me and
brought me back to you. Now, I am going to die paying the debt for what I have caused others to suffer.
I am back now like the prodigal son, ready to acknowledge that I have done wrong. Please don't send me
away." The father clasped his arms around his
daughter and held her to his breast.

The next day her father and mother overheard her
call "Irene" and went in to see what the trouble was.
The girl told them all about what had happened to
Irene and what part she played in the whole affair.
She could not rest or even close her eyes without see-

ing Irene.

"Irene, Irene, please get back and let me die! Please let me die."

About four o'clock that afternoon the girl said, "Thank God! Thank God! It is all over now. Whatsoever a man soweth so shall he reap." She called her mother and father, kissed them good-bye, and then passed away.

————————————

Mothers, train your children while they are young, so that when they grow old, they will not depart from it.

————————————

THE END.

GEORGE SAMPSON BRITE

GEORGE SAMPSON BRITE

By

ANNE SCOTT

PRO VERITATE
ET
PROGRESSIONE

BOSTON
MEADOR PUBLISHING COMPANY
MCMXXXIX

PRINTED IN THE UNITED STATES OF AMERICA

The Meador Press, Boston, Mass.

Note: The names of all persons and places are fictitious. The characters are fictitious. The plots are fictitious.

CONTENTS

7

GEORGE SAMPSON BRITE

GEORGE SAMPSON BRITE

"Miz Smith, Miz Herman sent George Sampson outa Music 'cause when we was singin' 'Th Ole Time Religun' he kept on pattin' his feet."

After dutifully delivering this message, Marjorie Moore, a trim little brown-skinned miss of nine years, looked up into the teacher's face to note the effect. Seeing from the manner in which Miss Smith was glaring down at George Sampson that the message had carried, Majorie raised up on her tip-toes, placed one arm/ around the teacher's neck and whispered, with one eye on George Sampson, "An' he said his mother was comin' over Thursdee and beat you up."

"I ain't said nuthin'," ejaculated George Sampson, "an' my mutha did say that, too."

Miss Smith, a tall slender, light brown-skinned young woman with well groomed black hair, had no toleration for foolishness. She drew herself up to her full height, folded her arms, looked sternly down on George Sampson Brite and demanded, "Boy! What do you mean by patting your feet!"

11

"That's d'way they does in church," grumbled George Sampson sulkily.

"Church! You're a good one to be talking about church. You were reported every day last week for poor conduct. Even Miss Ross, the apprentice teacher, reported you Friday for sliding down the bannisters an' here you are starting off again, Monday, first day in the week, with the same thing. Tell your mother I wish to see her."

"My mutha's at th' horspital," whimpered George Sampson.

"It's no wonder she's in the hospital having to be bothered with you," said Miss Smith.

"She ain't *in* th' horspital she jis work there an' she gits off on Thursdee aftanoon," grumbled George Sampson.

"Um-hum just write your name on the board an stay in the cloakroom until recess," ordered the teacher.

So George Sampson shuffled to the board grumbling and muttering to himself and scribbled his name, George Sampson Brite, in large illegible script across the entire front blackboard. The children looked at the board and at each other and kind of giggled and looked to see what the teacher was going to say. Miss Smith came in, paid no attention whatever to George Sampson, took her seat and went on with the lesson.

The children were so interested in their work that they soon forgot about George Sampson.

They were making designs to put on the baskets which they would eventually make for Christmas. The designs were in the first stages. The children had drawn a number of flower forms on a sheet of paper. From these they were working out various designs. Eventually each would select the best design and work it out to fit the shape of his basket. Each row in turn took the designs up to the teacher. The teacher corrected them and the children returned to their seats and continued with the work.

George Sampson was still messing around at the front board thinking with satisfaction that his mother was coming over "Thursdee" and beat the teacher up.

Miss Smith's room was located at the end of the second floor next to the stairway. The school was made up of three floors. On the first floor were five class rooms, the principal's office and the kindergarten, on the second floor were five class rooms, a teacher's rest room and a store room, on the third floor were six class rooms.

The school year comprised forty weeks and was divided into four quarters. Each grade comprised four quarters of ten weeks each. The quarters were designated as a, b, c, d; that is the children in the first quarter of the first grade were I-d, the second quarter I-c, the third quarter I-b, and the fourth quarter I-a. At the end of each ten weeks the quarter changed and those children who has passed in the previous quarter's work were promoted to the next quarter. Those who had not passed in the quarter's work were not promoted to the next quarter but repeated the work of the quarter in which they had failed. Each room had two quarters of a grade. Report cards were given out every five weeks or half quarter. The important promotions from room to room were made twice a year, in January or February and September as the graduation exercises were held twice a year. Often in June a whole room was graduated. Usually in the mid-year only one class.

On the third floor the rooms were divided into two departmental units with three rooms in each unit. On the second floor the three highest rooms, 7, 8, and 9 were arranged into a departmental unit. The schedule was carefully made out so that each subject received its allotted time. Miss Smith's room was No. 8, Grade 5-c and 5-d. Marjorie and George Sampson were both in the B. Class in Miss Smith's room—5-d. Miss Green's room was No. 9, Grade 4-a and 4-b, Miss Herman's room was No. 7, Grade 5-a and 5-b. Miss Hodges in No. 10 and the other rooms below operated on the all day plan, that is, the teacher taught all the subjects to one room of children.

Miss Smith taught Arithmetic and Drawing. Miss Herman taught Music and English. Miss Green taught Physical Training and Geography. Each teacher also taught Health and Science to her own home room group. The children stayed in their home rooms one hour in the morning, from 9 to 10, and one hour in the afternoon from 1:00 to 2:00.

However the district superintendent had been changed and the present one did not believe in the departmental plan for the children of the fourth and fifth grades. He thought that the younger children had difficulty in adjusting themselves to the different personalities and also that the younger children profited more by staying in one room where the teacher could correlate the subjects and give individual instruction where needed. So it was understood that the next quarter the three rooms on the second floor would go back to the all-day plan and the departmental plan would be used only on the third floor.

Miss Smith's room was a light, airy one with a large cloakroom in front. The cloakroom was in reality a little ante-room with a large window. In the center of the cloakroom were a small table and four small chairs. The entrance to Miss Smith's room was on the left side at the front. The door was a large square-like one with a square glass panel in it Three large windows on the opposite side of the room faced the door. Across the front and back of the room and on the left side with the door were blackboards. Between the windows also were small blackboard panels. Each child had a number over his coat hook in the cloakroom so he would know just where to place his wraps. On the wall were vivid pictures and in the window was a box of artificial flowers which looked almost real. Miss Smith was exceedingly fond of pictures and flowers.

The children worked diligently on their designs while George Sampson wrote his name in large letters across the front board. Miss Smith went on with the work. After a while she turned around to see what George Sampson was doing and seeing what she saw ordered George Sampson to, "Erase that—whatever it is, write smaller and write so it can be read, and simply write George *Brite.*"

The children smiled to themselves. George Sampson proceeded to stick his mouth out. He stood and looked sullen for a few minutes but no one paid any attention to him so he began to write and rewrite and erase and rewrite until he finally succeeded in improving matters a little. Miss Smith went on correcting designs and paid no attention to him. Finally she turned around and contemplated the board for a few seconds, then finally said, "Um-hum—now march yourself into that cloakroom an' there stay until recess an' perhaps you'll know how to act in Music hereafter—an' at recess I'll see more about you."

George Sampson shuffled into the cloakroom, wormed and squirmed, sat down on the table, played with the buttons on the children's coats and every now and then meowed like a cat.

Finally he came to the door, stuck his head out, stated that he was tired and made a face. The teacher paid no attention whatever to him.

The recess bell rang. The class that was in Miss Smith's room passed to Miss Herman's room and Miss Smith's home room children returned to her room, got their wraps and lined up for recess. Miss Smith watched George Sampson with an eagle eye to see that he did not slip out. After the lines had gone out George Sampson sided up to the door and peeped out to see what his chances were for slipping out. Just then Miss Smith came in and ordered him to "sit down." George Sampson went reluctantly to his seat, mumbled and grumbled and turned and twisted.

The bell rang for the children to come in from recess. The children went to their home rooms and put up their wraps. Miss Smith watched them as they passed in. The teachers stood on duty at the door whenever the lines came in or went out. Each teacher went out into the yard once a week at recess and noon to supervise the children. This was Miss Herman's day in the yard so Miss Smith was keeping an eye on Miss Herman's children until she came in.

The bell rang for the children to pass to their proper departmental rooms. As the children lined up, George Sampson, seeing that the teacher was not looking so closely, started pushing ahead of a boy in the line and so a kind of fight, not exactly a fight, but a pushing back and forth started and the teacher told George Sampson to go back into the cloakroom and stay until noon. George Sampson straggled reluctantly into the cloakroom; sat down on the little table, looked out of the window, got up and sat down again, discovered a book of funny paper characters, took out his pencil and some paper which he found in his pocket and began to draw pictures from the "funny paper book," as the children called it. After a while he became tired of drawing, stuck his head out of the door several times and shuffled around and around in the cloakroom. Finally the noon bell rang.

As George Sampson shuffled out of the cloakroom and got in the back of the line Miss Smith reminded him positively that she wished to see his mother.

"You gonna see hu all right 'nough," muttered George Sampson as he sauntered out.

He gave a loud whoop as the air struck his lungs, hopped a truck which conveyed him a part of the way home, kicked a tin can the rest of the way and went through the side gate and into the back door.

George Sampson lived about five blocks from the school, in a little three room house with a large yard around it, front, back and side. Each room, the front room, the kitchen and the middle room had a door of its own. A plank walk extended from the front gate all around the house to the kitchen door and back to the coal shed. On one side of the house was a large vacant lot full of trees and sunflowers and wild clover where June bugs, grasshoppers and butterflies reveled in the summer time. The front yard was enclosed by a picket fence with a picket gate which swung open and shut. George Sampson and his little sister, Lottie, loved to swing back and forth on the gate. The side fence, a strong board fence, which separated the yard from the vacant lot had a gate in it about midway. This gate was on a line with the kitchen door. Across the street was another large vacant lot opposite the lot next door to George Sampson's house. When going to school it was more convenient for George Sampson and Lottie to go out of the front gate and cut across the lot across the street. When coming home they usually came through both lots and through the side gate into the kitchen door. When the lot was muddy they came in the front gate. George Sampson often made a shorter cut still by cutting through both lots and hopping the fence. In good weather George Sampson and Lottie went home to lunch, in bad weather they took their lunches to school or bought them.

George Sampson began getting a pitiful look on his face as he went in the kitchen door. Granny, a dark, thin, white-haired personage was fixing the lunch at the kitchen sink in the corner. His little sister, Lottie, was standing looking on.

Lottie had not gone to school that day because she had a cold. Lottie was 3-d and in Miss Wray's room on the first floor.

"How'd Granny's boy git 'long t'day?" inquired his grandmother. "Did'y tell Lottie's teecha that she had a cold an' couldn't come to school t'day?"

George Sampson did not answer but stuck out his mouth, attempted to squeeze out a tear and whined, "That ole Miz Smith's still pickin' on me, come makin' me stay in the cloakroom till noon cause that ole Margree what's hu pet come tellin' hu a lotta stuff 'bout me what warn't so an she's alays makin' fun a my clothes an' callin' my writin' hen scratchin' an' things lak that an' said I warn't no count an' didn't hab no home trainin' an' said my mutha didn't teech me no mannas.—An' she say I ain't got good sense."

"You got jis as much sense as she's got," sympathized Granny.—"Well jis git 'long th' best you can an' whin y'come home this evenin' tell y'ma bout it and I bitchu she'll go ova there an' beat hu head in."

Mrs. Brite, a widow, stout, dark brown and capable looking, worked in a hospital and was the breadwinner of the family. She supported her two children and her mother. Granny stayed home and kept house and did quilting when she could get it to do. She always had the supper ready and "saw" to the children as Mrs. Brite went early and stayed late. On Thursday Mrs.

Brite got off at 12 o'clock and had the afternoon off.

George Sampson followed Granny's advice and got along the best he could. He was able to get through the afternoon without any serious mishap. He kept his mind on his lessons a little longer than usual and managed not to get into mischief but he was still peeved at what he termed being "picked on."

About six-thirty Mrs. Brite arrived home and placed her groceries and bundle of working clothes on the table and inquired of Granny, "Well Ma, how's things been goin' t'day?"

"O tol'able—tol'able," replied Granny, "but that ole teecha's still apickin' on George Sampson."

"Yessum she jis treated me awful t'day," complained George Sampson coming in from the middle room, "come makin' me stay in the cloak room 'cause hu pet tol hu a lotta stuff on me what warn't so and said she was gonna smack my head off—an' said I ain't got no sense."

"I'm sick an' tired a hu foolishness," declared Mrs. Brite indignantly—"always apickin' on my chile—my chile's jis as good as inybody else's chile an' got jis as much sense, too.—Now George Sampson jis try t'git along till Thursdee when I gits off. Then I'm goin' ova there an beat hu head in."

Things went fairly well the next day. George Sampson was on his "P's and Q's" in order to get out at recess to play ball. One of his class-mates and bosom friends, Thomas Brown, had brought a brand new ball and bat to school.

The following day was the last Wednesday of the month, the day on which Miss Herman, the Music and English teacher, always had a program consisting of solos, speeches and dances. The children marched single file to Miss Herman's room, took seats and the program started. The pupils always marched single file from one departmental room to another. When they were passing into and out of the yard they went in twos.

Helen Jenkins played a piano solo with many runs and trills, after which some of the children applauded too loudly and one boy whistled.

Miss Herman explained to them that it was perfectly all right to applaud but applause must be given in a refined manner. To make the point perfectly clear she had Helen Jenkins play the last section of the solo again, after which she illustrated to the children the proper manner in which to applaud. The children applauded in the manner indicated by Miss Herman.

The program continued. Samuel Jones played a violin solo and three children dramatized Dunbar's poem, "In the Morning." The class applauded in the manner prescribed by the teacher. The next number was a Spanish dance by Thelma Wells, a plump little miss, with black eyes and hair, dressed in a red and yellow Spanish costume.

She danced, turned, whirled around and beat the tambourines in real Spanish fashion. Marjorie played for Thelma to dance.

The children gave hearty but refined applause. George Sampson, however, was so elated that he could not contain himself. Instead of applauding in the manner approved by the teacher, he raised up in his seat and whooped, "Hot dog!"

The little girls looked from Miss Herman to George Sampson in duly horrified fashion. The boys wanted to do their duty by appearing shocked but they could not refrain from chuckling. Miss Herman looked severely at George Sampson and ordered, "Go to your home room an' don't come back."

George Sampson sauntered down the steps looking glum and grumbling to himself, "Nobodee can't neva hab no fun."

After a few minutes Miss Herman turned to Marjorie and said, "See if George Sampson has gone to Miss Smith's room an' tell Miss Smith I simply can't have that boy in my room. He's a disgrace.—Every time he comes in here there's trouble."

Marjorie was pleased to take the message and tripped to Miss Smith's room with nimble feet. George Sampson straggled to the home room, stood outside but did not venture in. He stood there toying with the Indian clubs which hung on the wall outside the door. Some time previously Indian clubs had been used for the Physical Training exercises. The use of Indian clubs in Physical Training had been discontinued. The "setting up" exercises were all "free hand." But the Indian clubs still hung around the walls and were sometimes used for games.

After a minute or so Marjorie came to bring the message from Miss Herman. George Sampson was toying with an Indian club as Marjorie passed by. Marjorie made a face at George Sampson as she passed by him. George Sampson shook the Indian club at her. Marjorie tossed her head scornfully into the air signifying that she knew he dare not bother her because she had a brother twice his size.

She tipped to the teacher's desk and whispered airily, "George Sampson's outside the door. He got sent outa Music for hollering, 'Hot dog' when Thelma did her Spanish dance."

Miss Smith's face clouded. Miss Herman's children who were in Miss Smith's room doing their design work looked up casually. They were used to hearing about George Sampson and did not wish to take up time from their designs to interest themselves in his performances.

Miss Smith began severely, "Sent out of Music again. I'm so sick an' tired of that boy I don't know what to do. Every time I turn around he's into one thing or another."

She went to the door and opened it with a sharp push. George Sampson stood guiltily toying with the Indian club and turning and twisting uneasily. "What do you mean by getting sent out of Music again?" demanded Miss Smith. "Every time I turn around I'm hearing about you.—What is the matter with you anyhow?—Put that Indian club up an' fix up that trouser leg.—You look like some I don't know what—all disconnected."

Miss Smith looked through the glass to see what the children were doing. The children were busy with their work. They were anxious to finish the designs so they could start the construction of the baskets. The construction work consisted of making the basket from strawboard and colored paper. After the basket was constructed the design was traced on it and painted. This kind of work was more or less individualized. Some children naturally worked faster than others and Miss Smith allowed each to progress at his own rate.

Mrs. Hopson, the matron, passed by, broom in hand, and looked amusedly at George Sampson.

"What is the matter with you?" continued Miss Smith.

"You ain't got no bizness makin' fun a'peeples clothes," mumbled George Sampson.

"Shut your mouth!—What do you mean by whooping an' yelling, 'Hot dog?'"

"Nuthin'."

"What!"

"I don mean nuthin'," mumbled George Sampson.

"Um-hum, well stay in here at recess an' learn how to act," commanded Miss Smith.

The children returned to their home rooms and passed out to recess.

Miss Smith took pains to see that George Sampson did not slip out during the recess period. George Sampson sat in his seat and twisted and turned and mumbled and grumbled. Finally the bell rang for the children to come in from recess.

George Sampson's class was scheduled to go to Miss Green's room after recess. This was the Physical Training day and as the weather was good the children expected to go out doors and play ball. George Sampson was a good ball player and captain of his team. The captains were elected by democratic vote. George Sampson was very anxious to go out and play with his team so he got over to one side where Miss Smith could not see him and be reminded of his conduct and attempted to go to the next room with the other children. Miss Smith spied him however and thinking that perhaps he would get into more mischief told him to go to his seat and stay in the room. "I'll write Miss Green a note," she said, "and tell her I'm keeping you. I'm sure she won't grieve over the matter."

"I don see why I can't play ball sometime lak otha peeple," grumbled George Sampson.

"Shut your mouth—I don't see why you can't do right like other people either. You'll get out in that yard an' the first thing I know you'll be starting up something else. Now just get out that geography book an' study that lesson that you don't know!" instructed Miss Smith.

George Sampson went reluctantly back to his seat and took out his geography book and pretended to be studying.

The class that came into Miss Smith's room paid no attention to George Sampson. They were too much interested in their arithmetic work. They were solving orally, problems without numbers and this always proved fascinating to them. Time hung heavily on George Sampson's hands. He fumbled and fiddled with his geography book, listened to the children working arithmetic problems and tried to fathom out what they were doing.

Then thoughts of vengeance filled his mind. He rejoiced to think that his mother was coming over to beat the teacher up. It seemed to him years before the bell rang for noon. At last the first bell rang and the children passed to their home rooms to get their wraps and pass out for the noon intermission.

As the children came into the home room to get their wraps Thomas told George Sampson that Sam Smith made the team lose. George Sampson punched Sam Smith slyly, so he thought, but it happened that Miss Smith was looking in his direction and ordered him to stay in at noon.

The children lined up. Miss Smith cautioned them to be back on time and come in with the lines. The lines came in at one o'clock but the children were not marked tardy until one-fifteen. The lines passed out for the noon intermission. As the lines were passing a boy handed Miss Smith a notice to read and sign. George Sampson seeing Miss Smith's attention diverted croutched down behind Thomas, Robert and Jesse Redd, another member of his team, ran home top speed and told his grandmother amid many crocodile tears, "That ole teecha's still pickin' on me. Made me stay in at recess for nuthin' an' wouldn't lemme play ball or nuthin' an' come tellin' me t'stay in at noon 'cause anotha boy hit me—but I come on home 'cause I was hongree."

Y'done right," answered Granny sympathetically. "Thim teechas makes me sick pickin' on peeples chillun. All they thinks 'bout is dressin' theyself up an' struttin' 'round with they nose stuck up puttin' on airs. Jis wait tilł t'morra whin yo Ma gits off—I bitchu she'll go ova there an' beat hu head in. Now jis stay home wid Granny an rest yo'self."

So George Sampson remained at home that afternoon and threw rocks and played ball and shot marbles to his heart's delight.

The next morning George Sampson reached school at nine-thirty and sauntered sheepishly into the room. He would have stayed home but he feared the truant officer, who had been after him several times on previous occasions. The children were busy with their arithmetic when he walked in.

Miss Smith looked up, saw George Sampson and ordered him to, "Stand outside the door," adding—"the idea of you having the nerve to cross this threshold after your actions of yesterday."

Miss Smith assigned the lesson in arithmetic. The children were finishing up the subject of addition of fractions. Miss Smith had placed eight examples in addition of fractions on the board. Each child had a large sheet of paper which he tore into eight pieces. On each piece of paper he placed one of the examples. When he had finished the first example he laid it aside and went on with the next one. Miss Smith marked the examples in order and handed them back. The children strove to see how many examples they could get right. The teacher jotted down the names of the children who did not seem to understand the examples so that she could come back to these children later and give them individual instruction.

The children began their work and Miss Smith stepped outside of the door to "see about" George Sampson.

George Sampson was shifting uneasily from one foot to another.

"Where were you at noon yesterday?" demanded Miss Smith, "I told you to stay in!"

"I was hongree," muttered George Sampson,

"an' I had t'go home an' eat, an' my mutha said she's comin' ova here t'day all right 'nough."

"Well she won't get here a minute too soon," observed the teacher, "an' if she isn't here this week I'm gonna know the reason why. March yourself into this room an' don't let me hear one word from you."

George Sampson stuck his mouth out about three inches, shuffled down the aisle to his seat, flopped down heavily, all the time mumbling to himself something to the effect that, "his mutha was coming over an' beat that ole hard-boiled teecha up." Some of the children who heard the remark looked wide-eyed at George Sampson and then at the teacher to see if she had heard the remark. According to the look on the teacher's face she evidently had heard nothing.

Sophie Campbell, a plump energetic little girl, seated near enough to overhear the remark got out of her seat and tip-toed conscientiously up to the teacher and whispered in her ear repeating what George Sampson had said.

"Um-hum is that so?" inquired Miss Smith with a dark look at George Sampson and then went on with the lesson. The children passed up Example No. 1. The teacher marked and returned it and followed the same procedure with the rest of the examples. Those children who got all of the examples right were highly elated and piled them up in a neat pile to take home.

The bell rang for the classes to change. Miss

Smith's room passed to Miss Green for Geography
while Miss Green's room came to Miss Smith for
Arithmetic. Miss Smith, as usual, cautioned the
children to have good lessons and conduct and no
bad reports.

The geography class had just completed the
topic, "Why New England is a great manufactur-
ing center." Miss Green had planned a test upon
the topic just finished. The paper was passed and
the children began eagerly to answer the questions
because Miss Green had an honor roll on the
wall upon which she would place the names of
those who had a good mark on the test.

George Sampson sat for a full ten minutes making figures on the desk. Finally he condescended
to consume one-half of the paper with his full
name, George Sampson Brite. He looked at the
questions on the board and seeing none to his
liking took out his page from the funny paper
and drew a picture of a cowboy.

Miss Green, suspecting George Sampson of ir-
regularities, went to the window, adjusted the
shade, came casually around by George Sampson's
seat took hold of his paper and examined it.

"Where is your work?" she asked.

"I ain't got none," grumbled George Sampson,
"I done f'got all that stuff an' b'sides I warn't
here."

"You were here," asserted Miss Green, "an'
in the first place why do you write your name all
over the paper an' what has this picture to do

with the test? There's Miss Smith passing the door now. Thelma, ask her to step inside a minute please."

Miss Smith came in looking inquiringly at the children and said, "Good morning, Miss Green."

"Good morning, Miss Smith," answered Miss Green. "I wish you would look at this boy's paper. This is what he's done in twenty minutes—name all over the paper—no room for anything else an' look at that picture."

"What is this?" exclaimed Miss Smith taking hold of the paper and reading it.

George Sampson grumbled something.

"Just keep your mouth shut," ordered Miss Smith, "an' stay in at noon until you learn how to act."

Miss Smith returned to her room. Shortly the bell rang for the children to pass back to their home rooms preparatory to the noon intermission. George Sampson attempted to slip out down behind some members of his team, but Marjorie saw him and immediately informed Miss Smith. Miss Smith spotted him and ordered him back to his seat. So George Sampson stayed in his seat until 12:30 looking glum at what he termed being picked on, but with a feeling of satisfaction in knowing that his mother would soon be over to settle the score.

At 12:30 he set out for home pondering upon his wrongs that would soon be avenged. He cut across the lot, burst in through the side gate and on in through the kitchen door. As it was Thursday his mother was off for the afternoon. As soon as he got into the kitchen he began shedding crocodile tears.

"What's d'matta wid you boy?" demanded Mrs. Brite in alarm.

"Well what on earth!" exclaimed Granny as she looked up from where she was sitting by the kitchen sink peeling potatoes.

"That ole mean, hard-boiled teecha's still pickin' on me," wept George Sampson. "Come makin' fun a me an said I don know nuthin' an' ain't got no sense. An' she wouldn't lemme go out an' play ball an' she let all th' otha children go out an' play ball an' they acted worsin' me. An' a lil' ole gal name Margee what's hu pet, she b'lieves everythin' she says an' she's alays makin' up things 'bout me an' tellin' hu. An she tol hu I was cheatin' in gography an' she came fussin' at me an' made me stay in at noon."

"Well you got jis as much sense as she is," retorted his mother.

"Sho is," piped up Granny from where she sat in the corner. "Sho is."

"I'm sick an' tired a hu pickin' on my chile," went on Mrs. Brite, "an' this here is th' day I said I was goin' after hu an' I'm a goin', too."

Granny nodded her head approvingly.

"She lits thim otha peeple's chil'rin do as they pleases an' picks on my George Sampson," raved

Mrs. Brite. "I ain't gonna stand f'it no longer. I'm goin' ova there an' bust hu in hu mouth."

Granny continued to nod approval.

The one o'clock bell had just rung. Miss Smith was standing just outside of her door supervising the passing in of lines. In a few minutes the lines were all in and Miss Smith was preparing to go into the room when George Sampson and his mother appeared on the scene.

"That's hu," whispered George Sampson indicating Miss Smith, as they came up the steps.

Mrs. Brite swaggered forward and demanded in loud tones, "Is you Miss Smith?"

"Good afternoon Madam," answered the teacher as she pushed the door of her room shut. "Yes I'm Miss Smith. I presume that you're George Sampson's mother. Well I'm sorry to say that George Sampson's conduct has been very poor."

"His connuck ain't been no poorer'n nobody elses," contradicted Mrs. Brite in loud tones, "you jis got a pick on my chile—my chile's jis as good as inybody elses chile an' b'sides he's got jis as much sense too, an' you an' nobody else ain't got no bizness makin' fun a him an' callin' him crazy."

"Madam I think you had better see the principal," advised Miss Smith coldly.

"I ain't studin' th' principal," yelled Mrs. Brite, "my bizness is wid you an' I come ova here to show you how to quit pickin' on my George Sampson. So saying she made a threatening launch toward the teacher and raised her right arm in a menacing manner.

The children, hearing the loud tones crowded to the door and peered through the glass. Miss Green and Miss Herman stepped to their doors to see what was going on. Mrs. Hopson, the matron, stepped up, broom in hand, to see what the trouble was.

George Sampson stepped up briskly behind his mother when she launched forward.

Miss Smith stepped agily to one side and coldly taking hold of one of the Indian clubs from the wall stood in readiness to meet further advances from the enemy.

She took one step back and Mrs. Brite's eyes grew large. George Sampson's eyes bulged and his mouth hung open. Mrs. Brite waved her hand to one side saying, "Now Miz Smith I didn't come here t'start up no fussin' an' fightin' wid no teechas. I'm a peacable woman, I am. I sends George Sampson t'school t'do what y'all tells him an' ef he don do it I wants t'know. Look here George Sampson git outa my sight be'fo I lands on you right now! Well I'll see you some mo Miz Smith. Good-bye."

"Good-bye Mrs. Brite."

GEORGE SAMPSON'S REVENGE

Tuesday morning came, a dreary, misty November day. George Sampson shut the picket gate and put the rope fastener over it and the post of the fence as he and Lottie waved Granny "Goodbye" and went down the board sidewalk, across the street and across the lot.

As they trudged across the lot they talked about the show which the Patrons' Association was to hold on the following Saturday morning.

"Say I bet they gonna hab a Wild West Show Sat'day," effervesced George Sampson. "I wish't I could git a free ticket—I sho do."

"Yeh—that would be nice," replied Lottie, "but how could you get one?"

"I donno," pondered George Sampson, "but I sho wish't I could git one."

"Well I'm gonna try to sell ten an get one free," mused Lottie.

"I don wanta sell ten," complained George Sampson, "but I sho wish't I could git one free."

As they continued across the barren lot George Sampson stooped down and picked up something.

"Oh George Sampson, put that looking glass down!" exclaimed Lottie. "It's cracked all the way across. It's bad luck! Everybody says it's bad luck you know. But it can't fall out cause the frame's too tight but it's bad luck just the same."

"Yeh, I know it's bad luck," replied George Sampson, "but I'm gonna keep it an' put it in Margree's desk an give hu bad luck 'cause she's alays tellin' th' teecha on me an gittin' me in trouble. I wish't she was a boy so I could bust hu in the nose. But I'm gonna put this ole cracked lookin' glass in hu desk an' give hu bad luck all right 'nough."

"That's right," approved Lottie, "ole Margree sure thinks she's cute 'cause she's got them little ole plaits an takes music lessons. She sure thinks she's cute an' betta than other people an' tries to talk proper an' be th' teacher's pet."

"Yeh," repeated George Sampson. "I'm gonna put it in hu desk an' give hu bad luck."

They trudged along for a few minutes in silence. George Sampson felt in his pocket to see if he had a pencil and pulled out an eraser with a little brush on it.

"Oh George Sampson, where did you get that nice eraser with that brush on it?" questioned Lottie as George Sampson dropped the eraser and picked it up again.

"Miz Hopson gimme this raser th' otha day when I went to git hu lunch for hu," explained George Sampson turning the eraser over and looking at it. "Somebodee gave it to hu an' she saved it for me. She saves me a lotta things 'cause I gits hu lunch for hu. Next time she gives me a raser I'm gonna save it for you."

Every day George Sampson went to the store across the street to get Mrs. Hopson's lunch for her. Even on days when he went home he got the lunch before he went home. Mrs. Hopson always had a boy to get her lunch. She kept him as long as he proved reliable and regular. When he became careless she got another boy and kept him as long as he proved reliable.

At present George Sampson was the matron's "lunch-getter."

Another turn of the corner and George Sampson and Lottie reached school and entered by way of the front door. The school building had three entrances, a front door and two side doors. In the morning before 8:30 boys and girls both went in the front door. After 8:30 and at recess and noon the boys went in and out of the west side door and the girls in and out of the east side door.

Next door to the school was a large vacant lot which had been leased for use as a school playground. The children went on the playground in the morning, and at noon. George Sampson usually went on the playground every morning and played until the last minute.

"Ain't you goin' on th' playground, George Sampson?" asked Lottie as George Sampson came on in the front gate along with her.

"No," replied George Sampson, "th' 8:30 bell's ringing an' I'm goin' on up to th' room an' do what I tol you. Be sho an' wait for me at noon."

"All right," replied Lottie.

George Sampson went on up into his room. The children were moving around sharpening pencils, looking over their spelling words, studying their arithmetic tables and otherwise improving the time. The teacher allowed them a little freedom from 8:30 until 8:45 but at 8:45 every child was required to be in his own seat and about his "morning work." In the bustle and stir of things George Sampson moved down the aisle toward the pencil sharpener and slipped the said looking glass into Marjorie's desk. Nobody paid any attention to him and if they had they would have thought that he merely picked up something which had fallen on the floor.

George Sampson went on to the pencil sharpener, sharpened his pencil and went on back to his "morning work," at the same time keeping an eye open to see if Marjorie came in.

At 8:45 the bell rang for the children to come in. An early room for children who came before 8:30 was kept by the teachers each in turn, beginning with the Room One teacher. At 8:30 the children were dismissed from the early room. Some went to the playground, some went out into the school yard to play while others went to their regular rooms to look over their lessons and get a little head start for the day. At 8:45 the bell rang for all the children to go to their regular rooms. During the period 8:45-9:00 the children did what was termed "morning work." This consisted mostly of different forms of review work. The type of "morning work" was decided upon by the individual teacher. Miss Smith usually made use of review arithmetic. On this particular morning the children had been given four examples in long multiplication which they were to work and prove by interchanging the multiplier and the multiplicand. Promptly at 9 o'clock, when the tardy bell rang, the "morning work" papers were collected. These papers were marked and the grades put on the "morning work" chart which the teacher kept hanging on the wall. At 9 o'clock the children were marked tardy.

The children always tried to be at school at 8:45 so that they would have time to do their "morning work" and consequently get a good mark on the chart. By means of the chart each child could see his own improvement and his standing in relation to each other member of the class. So George Sampson was working away at his "morning work" and waiting for developments in the looking glass case.

When the 8:45 bell rang and the lines came in Marjorie was not with them. George Sampson grew anxious. Five minutes passed. The children were working diligently at their arithmetic but Marjorie had not yet appeared.

George Sampson grew more and more anxious lest his plan fail to carry.

"Good mornin' Miz Smith," said Mrs. Hopson, the matron, as she came in to wipe the window sills.

"Good morning Mrs. Hopson," answered Miss Smith.

The children went on busily with their work while Miss Smith arranged the things on her desk. George Sampson was working with one eye on his work and one eye on the door. He was watching to see if Marjorie came—but no Marjorie. Another three minutes passed and then about five minutes to nine Marjorie rushed in breathless, hat and lunch and little pocketbook in hand with a note from her mother saying:

"Dear Miss Smith,
         I had to send Marjorie on an errand. Will you please let her do her morning work at recess so she won't have a poor mark on the chart. She is so worried about it.
                              From her mother
                              Mrs. Moore."

"Yes Marjorie," replied Miss Smith after reading the note, "you may do your morning work at recess since you brought a note from your mother."

The children were not allowed to do their

"morning work" at recess or noon except for good reason. One of the main purposes of the morning work was to get the children to school on time. However, upon bringing a note from his parent a child was allowed to do his "morning work" at noon or recess.

George Sampson dallied with his work and watched and waited while Marjorie took her seat. She sat down daintily and placed her lunch and hat and pocketbook in her desk, took out her wax crayon box, got out her pencil and eraser, and placed them on the top of her desk; then reached back and got her pencil bag and a few pieces of scrap paper but no discovery was made of the said looking glass.

Marjorie sat in the front seat in the outside row nearest the door. George Sampson sat in the third seat in the outside row nearest the window and fartherest from the door. His seat had been moved a number of times and this was his latest location.

The 9 o'clock bell rang, the children in each row passed their papers up to the child in the front seat. One little girl collected the papers from the front seats and gave them to the teacher who placed them in a book file, which she kept on her desk, until she was ready to mark them.

George Sampson kept eyeing Marjorie but no results in the looking glass case.

Miss Smith told the children to look on the floor and pick up any scrap paper that might be there. Miss Smith constantly cautioned the children to keep the floor clean.

After the arithmetic papers had been duly collected and the scrap paper on the floor removed Miss Smith asked the children who had sold tickets for the show to raise their hands.

The Patrons' Association was planning a Benefit Show to be held two weeks from the following Saturday. The proceeds of the show were to be used for the purpose of purchasing a radio for the school. The children were assisting the Patrons' Association by selling tickets. One of the moving picture theatres in the neighborhood had donated everything for the occasion. The show was to be held from 9 A.M. to 11 A.M. Each room, of course, wanted to make a good showing in ticket selling. The tickets were ten cents each. Each child who sold ten tickets was given a free ticket.

Several children raised their hands in response to Miss Smith's question. Miss Smith took out her notebook and envelope and made a record of the tickets sold. She then urged the children to try and sell their tickets so that their room would have a good showing.

Then she asked Mrs. Hopson, who was wiping the glass in the door, if she had bought her ticket yet.

"Yes'm," replied Mrs. Hopson, stopping her work and turning around, glad of the opportunity to have something to say. "I bought a ticket for the benefit of th' children but I can't go 'cause I have to work till twelve o'clock on Saturday."

"Well we're very sorry you can't go but we're glad you bought a ticket," replied Miss Smith.

"Goody-goody, I'm gonna ask hu to gimme that ticket when I go to git hu lunch so I kin hab a free ticket," thought George Sampson to himself with much satisfaction.

"Now," said Miss Smith, "those who didn't have a ticket report to-day try an' have a ticket report next time. Now if there are no more ticket reports B. Class take out your arithmetic notebooks and take out the paper you had yesterday. A. Class you will find your work on the front board."

The B. Class took out their arithmetic notebooks and got out the papers they had prepared on the previous day. These papers contained original problems involving addition of fractions. The problems had been composed by the children themselves. The A. Class was composing ten original problems involving subtraction of fractions.

The children kept certain arithmetic papers in notebooks so the papers could be easily referred to. The teacher marked the most important papers and returned them to the children. The children corrected these papers and put them into their notebooks. They also kept any other important arithmetic papers in the notebook.

George Sampson watched with suspense as Marjorie went into her desk to take out her arithmetic notebook. Nothing happened. Marjorie placed the notebook daintily on the desk, removed the paper then folded her hands. Miss Smith called on Thelma to read one of her original problems. Thelma read the problem. The children worked it. Another child then gave one of his original problems for the class to work. The same procedure followed until the arithmetic period was over. The children enjoyed the recitation immensely.

At the end of the recitation period the teacher had the papers collected and passed out mimeographed sheets with ten graded problems in subtraction of fractions on them. The children were to work these problems and place them in their notebooks for the next day's recitation.

The A. Class gave out their original problems in the same manner that the B. Class had done.

At the end of the arithmetic period the Health books were passed out to both classes and the teacher had a child write on the board the directions that were to be followed. The children were to read the chapter on "Prevention of Disease," fold their papers into four parts and make a chart showing eight ways in which to prevent disease and write one sentence explaining each point.

Shortly the bell rang for the children to prepare for recess. The children placed all books and materials in their desks, removed all paper from the floor and passed row by row to get their wraps.

The second bell rang and the children lined up, each row in its turn, girls in the side aisle and boys in the rear aisle.

"Marjorie, you may stay in at recess an' do your morning work if you like since you brought a note," said Miss Smith.

"Yes'm," replied Marjorie.

The third bell rang, the lines passed out but Marjorie had not yet uncovered the said looking glass.

In the course of the recess activities George Sampson grabbed Roy's, a kind of timid boy's hat and ran over by the fence between the boys' yard and the girls' yard. Roy started off to tell the teacher and George Sampson threw the hat at him.

"Yoo-hoo, George Sampson," called his little sister through the fence. George Sampson turned around and went over near Lottie.

"Did you put that ole lookin' glass in Margree's desk yet?" whispered Lottie.

"Yeh but she ain't found it yet," answered George Sampson, "you know what," he continued with enthusiasm, "Miz Hopson ain't gonna use hu ticket to th' Show 'cause she's gotta work on Sat'day an' I'm gonna ask hu t'give it to me when I go to git hu lunch an' I'm sho she'll give it to me 'cause she laks me."

"I hope she does," said Lottie. "I sure hope she does."

"Be sho an' wait f'me at noon y'hear," called

George Sampson as the bell rang for the children to line up.

Lottie did not always wait for George Sampson. Sometimes she went on home.

The children passed back into their various rooms. After they had settled down Miss Smith had Sam pass out two sets of supplementary geography books from which the children were to prepare their geography lessons. Each child had two supplementary books beside the regular geography text. A number of other geography books were on the library table. The children were to consult these books, make an outline, and write compositions in their own words. The B. Class had for their subject, "The Occupations of the People of Alaska," while the A. Class had for their subject, "The Strange Manners and Customs of the People of India."

George Sampson was working half heartedly with one eye on Marjorie. Time passed. He was beginning to despair lest Marjorie would not find the looking glass in question and have bad luck as he had planned. He was about to give up hope when he looked in Marjorie's direction and saw how diligently she was working with her books. In the course of her work Marjorie looked into her desk to get out her eraser. Evidently Marjorie had difficulty in finding the eraser. She fumbled and felt all around in her desk. George Sampson looked with renewed interest and hope. In the course of her search Marjorie pulled out something irrevelant, the looking glass. She looked at it and turned it over and behold, it was cracked all the way across.

George Sampson's heart leaped with joy as Marjorie gazed at and turned over the cracked looking glass undecided what to do.

Finally she rose daintily from her seat, tip-toed up to the teacher's desk in a very prim and proper manner and said, "Miss Smith, may I take this cracked looking glass down to the matron to dispose of because it's dangerous to put any kind of glass in the waste can. Some one might get hurt."

"Dispose of," whispered George Sampson to himself, "tryin' to talk proper, tee-hee she jis learnt that word."

"Yes indeed," replied Miss Smith, "that's right, never put any glass in the waste can because someone might be injured. Always be considerate of other people."

So Marjorie tipped very conscientiously down the steps to the matron's room and began, "Miz Hopson, I brought this ole cracked looking glass down to you to dispose of—I didn't put it in the waste can 'cause I thought you might cut your hand on it, or something."

"Oh how sweet of you to think 'bout me," ejaculated Mrs. Hopson, highly pleased. "So you don want me to cut my hand—well that's awful sweet of you. Lemme see—hab'y bought yo ticket to th' Show yet?"

Marjorie replied that she had not.

"Well now here," said Mrs. Hopson, reaching in her desk, "you kin hab my ticket 'cause I ain't goin'. I can't go I hab to work till twelve o'clock Saturday—an' tell Miz Smith you is jis as nice as you kin be."

So Marjorie went back to her room in high spirits. She put the ticket in her little pocketbook and went about her work with great satisfaction.

George Sampson looked over at Marjorie, ducked his head down and laughed to himself thinking of the bad luck in store for her.

The children worked diligently on their compositions. Miss Smith walked around, looked at the work and gave suggestions and helpful criticisms.

The first bell rang. The children put up their materials, passed and got their wraps preparatory to going out for the noon intermission.

As Marjorie's row passed to get their wraps George Sampson looked on with satisfaction. The children lined up to pass out and the teacher cautioned them about their conduct on the street.

George Sampson hurried down to the matron's room to find out what she wanted from the store and to get the ticket for the Show.

"Now lemme see George Sampson," began Mrs. Hopson taking out her pocketbook, "get me a frank san'wich an' a dimes worth of chile."

"Yessum," replied George Sampson and then hesitated and asked timidly, "Miz Hopson if you ain't gonna go to th' show will you gimme yo ticket what you bought?"

"Why George Sampson," said Mrs. Hopson regretfully, "I wish't youda asked me sooner, I wish't you hada—but I gave my ticket to Marjorie on accounta she was so nice to me an' wouldn't put that ole cracked lookin' glass in the can on accounta I might cut my hand. But next time I hab a ticket I'm gonna save it for you sho.—I sho am."

"Yessum," replied George Sampson backing out, dazed, surprised and out-done.

His little sister was waiting at the gate and asked eagerly, "Did Margree find that ole lookin' glass, did you git th' ticket, George Sampson?"

"Yeh, she found the lookin' glass but I ain't got no ticket," lamented George Sampson kicking an ice cream carton. "That old Margree's got 'nine lives.' Next time I find a cracked lookin' glass I'm gonna keep it for myself."

GEORGE SAMPSON AND THE
COAL MAN

Wednesday morning—8:15 A.M. The weather
was cloudy and cold as the weather man had for-
cast. George Sampson and his little sister started
off to school as usual. They had their lunches under
their arms. On days when the weather was bad
and when Granny went to her Sewing Circle they
always took their lunches. At other times they
went home to lunch.

"Now come straight home," cautioned Granny,
"an' I'll be here 'bout 4:30. I'll have th' dinna
all done. Y'know this is my Sewing Circle day.
Lottie is yo got th' key 'round yo neck good an'
strong?—Now George Sampson don play 'long th'
street an' study yo lesson an' practice yo writin'
an' write pretty. Yo see how nice Lottie writes
an' yo is five whole rooms ahead of hu."

George Sampson and Lottie reached school
just as the first bell rang. The children put up
their wraps, took their seats and went about the
"morning work."

After the children were seated Marjorie raised
her hand very demurely.

"What is it Marjorie?" asked Miss Smith.

Marjorie stood up by her seat and began, "This
morning that coal man that has an' ice an' coal

place around the corner was pushing coal an'
wood down th' alley an' hollering 'Coal' an George
Sampson kept mocking him an' hollering 'Coal'
real funny. An' the coal man got mad an' was
gonna do something to George Sampson an'
George Sampson ran an' hid behind the post an'
told the coal man to come and get him an' the coal
man was mad an' said, just wait till he gets his
hands on George Sampson he's gonna beat him
good an' then George Sampson ran around the
side of the alley an' made a face at the coal man."

"I ain't did nuthin," ejaculated George Sampson.

"You did so," returned Marjorie, "an' yesterday evenin' he scratched on the coal man's slate
where the people write how much coal and wood
they want an' the preacher that has the little
church next door where the store used to be told
George Sampson he ought not to do that an' just
then the coal man came out and asked some girls
who scratched on his slate an' they said 'George
Sampson.' An' George Sampson ran an' the coal
man said just wait till he gets his hands on George
Sampson an' he's gonna beat him good."

"Sho did," verified Sam Smith, the boy who sat
behind George Sampson, " 'cause I live right
across th' street from th' coal man an' I was on
my way to th' store 'cause I go to th' store every
evening soon's I get home from school an' I
heard th' coal man say it 'cause he was mad an'
he was talking real loud an' everybody was look-

ing. An' one day when the coal man had the
baskets of wood and coal piled up George Sampson knocked some of them over an' the coal man's
brother said he was gonna tell the coal man to
beat George Sampson good."

George Sampson turned around and gave Sam
Smith a menacing look. George Sampson considered Sam Smith his natural enemy because
Sam Smith was in charge of the ball and bat and
Physical Training apparatus which the children
used for their Physical Education lessons. That
is, Sam Smith saw to it that the ball and bat and
bean bags were kept in their proper places in the
case. Whenever they were to be used for a lesson
he got them out and put them back. When the
class went out in the yard for Physical Training
Sam carried the ball and bat. At times when
children from other rooms came to borrow the
apparatus he marched to the case and got it,
handed it over to the borrower and saw to it that
the apparatus was back in the room and in the
case at the proper time.

This was a sore point with George Sampson because his heart's desire was to be in charge of the
ball and bat and Physical Training apparatus. He
had been in charge of it for a few weeks but his
conduct had been such that the teacher took the
honor away from him and bestowed it on Sam
Smith. So George Sampson felt that Sam Smith
was his natural enemy.

When Sam Smith backed up what Marjorie

had said, George Sampson turned around and gave Sam a menacing look and shook his fist at him on the sly meaning that he was going to get even with him at the first opportune time.

"Now," began Miss Smith, "you must never tease people because that's a bad thing to do. It often leads to trouble. Numbers of people have gotten into serious trouble that way. Lots of people have started up serious trouble just by teasing people. Now I don't want to hear any more bad reports today because this is my birthday an' I think everybody should act nice—don't you?"

George Sampson tucked his head down and laughed and whispered, "I bet she's a hundred years ole."

Sophie Campbell overheard the remark and tipped up to the teacher and whispered, "Miss Smith, George Sampson said he bet you was a hundred years old."

"No—two hundred," replied Miss Smith as she moved toward the door to see if any children were loitering in the hall and incidently to have a word with Miss Green, the teacher in the next room.

"Cold isn't it?" remarked Miss Green.

"Yes it is," replied Miss Smith," and yesterday it was so cold in Miss Herman's room that she had to go in Miss Hodges' room an' stay all day."

"Miss Herman has a leave of absence to go away an' study music next year," informed Miss Green, "that'll be nice won't it? I'd like to go away an' study myself but I can't go just now."

"That certainly will be nice," agreed Miss Smith.

George Sampson, seeing that the teacher's attention was not directly on him took advantage of the opportunity. He turned around in his seat, shook his fist slyly at Sam Smith and threatened, "Wait till I git you. I'm gonna bust you in the nose."

Sam Smith said, "Yo Ma."

"Yo Gramma," retorted George Sampson, and then added, "all right now.—Y'talkin' 'bout my Mamma ain't'y? I'm gonna git'y f'that."

Miss Smith looked over the room to see how things were going and if all the children were at work. George Sampson and Sam Smith saw the teacher looking in their direction and pretended to be deep in their "morning work."

The 9 o'clock bell rang. The teacher closed the door and had the "morning work" papers collected. Tiny snowflakes began to fall and piled up on the window sill.

"Oh goody it's snowin'," effervesced George Sampson rising up in his seat.

The teacher gave him a severe look and he settled back down.

The tiny snowflakes gradually become larger and by recess time the ground was well covered with snow and the snow was still falling fast.

About ten o'clock the principal sent around a notice to the effect that they would have indoor

recess, that is, the children would go to the basement and come directly back to their rooms.

The children passed to the basement, each room
in its turn, the lowest room first. Sam Smith and
his partner were directly in front of George Sampson and his partner. The patrol boys stood on the
landings to see that order was maintained on the
stairs. The principal stood on the first floor at
the entrance to the basement. The teachers were
stationed at various points. Miss Smith cautioned
the children to go down the steps quietly and
orderly and come back up the steps quietly and
orderly and to keep with the same partner and
in the same place in the line coming up. Everything
went well going down but as they were turning
the first landing on the way back up George Sampson slyly gave Sam Smith a punch. Sam Smith
turned around and struck George Sampson a
telling blow. The patrol boy stopped them, took
them both out of the line and reported them to
Miss Smith.

"What do you mean by starting a fight on the
steps when I told you plainly to be careful of your
conduct?" demanded the teacher of both boys.

"George Sampson hit me first," protested Sam
Smith.

The patrol boy verified the statement saying,
"Yes'm I saw him punch Sam Smith in the back."

The teacher gave George Sampson a severe
look and demanded, "What do you mean by hitting

that boy after I told you to watch your conduct going down and coming up the steps?"

"He was talkin' 'bout my Mamma," protested George Sampson sticking out his mouth, "an' that petroleum boy don lak me nohow. That's why he took sides wid Sam."

"I presume you mean patrol boy," corrected the teacher. "Petroleum is oil that comes out of the ground that gasoline an' kerosene an' such things are made from. We studied about that in geography. If you had been paying attention to your geography lesson you would know about that. Now you say Sam was talking about your parent. What did he say?"

"He said, 'Yo Ma,'" asserted George Sampson.

"An' you said, 'Yo Gramma,'" declared Sam Smith.

"What statement did he make about your parent?" went on Miss Smith attempting to get into the details. "What did he say? When you talk about somebody you have to say something about them. You have to make some statement."

"He ain't said no stakement he jis said 'Yo Ma,'" ejaculated George Sampson.

"An' you said 'Yo Gramma,'" remonstrated Sam Smith.

"Well you can't talk about a person without making a statement or saying something," explained Miss Smith. "Is he acquainted with your parent? Does he know your parent?"

"No'am," replied George Sampson.

"And is he acquainted with your grandparent?" asked the teacher of Sam.

"No'am," replied Sam.

"Then how can you talk about someone you're not acquainted with?"

Neither made any reply.

"Now don't let me hear any more about this," instructed Miss Smith pointing her finger severely at each one. "You attend to your business an' you attend to yours. An' don't let me hear any more about this Y'Ma or Y'Gramma business. Do you understand?"

"Yes'm," replied both.

"Now Sam you change seats with John," said Miss Smith.

"George Sampson say he's gonna beat me up after school," complained Sam.

"You just let me hear of you fighting on that street or having any misconduct," warned Miss Smith shaking her finger austerely at George Sampson "that's all I have to say. Just let me hear of you having any misconduct on that street an' you'll wish you hadn't."

"I ain't said that," grumbled George Sampson, "I ain't said nuthin'."

"Just keep still an' look on the board an' find your work," directed Miss Smith.

According to the instructions on the board the children were to make an illustration of some winter sport. The children delighted in doing this kind of work especially on a snowy day.

George Sampson was secretly planning to "beat up" Sam Smith after school but as he turned the plan over in his mind he feared that he might be sent home the next day and have to bring his mother to school and he did not want to have to bring his mother again above all things because his mother had told him emphatically that she had better not have to go over to that school again. As he slowly drew the picture frame around his paper and looked out of the window at the snow falling he began to plan how he could "get" Sam Smith without any come-back on himself. As he watched the snow flakes twirling and whirling an idea began to slowly unfold itself. Yes he would snow ball Sam good but not right after school because that would bring on complications and get him in trouble with the teacher and he might have to bring his mother. So he thought and thought as to how he could "get" Sam Smith and still keep within the law.

At last an idea struck him. He reviewed the situation mentally. They would get out at three o'clock because of the bad weather. His mother would get home about 6:30. His grandmother had gone to her Sewing Circle and would not get home until 4:30. His little sister, Lottie, had taken the key around her neck. If he were late getting home his grandmother would be none the wiser and his little sister would not tell on him because he would tell her about Sam Smith and she would want him to "get" Sam Smith. As he watched the snow piling up the plan continued to unfold in his mind. He would wait until the boy got home and started to the store. Then he would snow ball him good and the teacher couldn't say anything because the boy would have been home first and that would take the case from under the jurisdiction of the school because according to his interpretation the jurisdiction of the school ended when you reached home. He did not think in terms of the word jurisdiction because that word was not in his vocabulary but that was the sum and substance of his thought.

Yes, he would wait until the boy got home and started to the store. Then he would snow ball him good and the teacher couldn't say anything because it would be after the jurisdiction of the school had ceased. So George Sampson contemplated the plan with relish as he sat looking at the snow flakes coming down and piling up on the window sill. He pictured himself making a good hard snow ball and zopping Sam Smith alongside the head. The only thing that annoyed him was the thought he would have to clean off the snow when he got home and cleaning off snow was the bane of his existence.

The afternoon passed serenely enough. The snow outside made things feel more cozy and comfortable within. A large number of children were absent, and the inclement weather program was on. The children were especially fond of the inclement weather program. They read from library books and drew with wax crayons and told stories.

The school day closed. The children got their wraps and lined up for dismissal. The snow had stopped falling. The snow on the ground was about three inches deep but the weather was not so very cold.

The teacher cautioned the children not to have any misconduct on the street and not to throw snow balls.

"Now remember, no snowballing!" was Miss Smith's last warning with a meaning look at George Sampson.

The lines passed out each in its turn. George Sampson's little sister, Lottie, was waiting for him at the gate.

"Lissen here, Lottie," commenced George Sampson as he and his little sister began to trudge along together taking pains to step in the deepest snow, "that ole Sam come saying 'Yo Ma' to me an' I hit him comin' up th' steps an' he tol th' teecha an' that ole petroleum boy tol th' teecha that it was my fault an' th' teecha said I betta not do nuthin' to Sam but I'm gonna git him all right 'nough. I'm gonna wait till he gits home an' then goes to th' store an' then I'm gonna snowball him good an' that ole Miz Smith can't say nuthin' 'cause he's already been home an' she won't hab nuthin' t'do wid it an he can't say nuthin' 'bout that 'cause he's already been home an' th' teecha won't hab nuthin' t'do wid it an' he can't go tellin' hu."

"That's right, that's right," approved Lottie, "git him good 'cause he ain't got no bizness sayin' 'Yo Ma.' "

"Now you go an' head home Lottie," George Sampson instructed, "an' don tell Granny nuthin' 'bout it 'cause it ain't no need for hu t'know an' I'll be home before she gits home from th' Sewing Circle."

"Yeh, all right," agreed Lottie, "I won't tell Granny nuthin' an' git him good 'cause he ain't got no bizness saying 'Yo Ma.' "

Lottie went on home. George Sampson peeped into the coal man's ice and coal wagon which was standing outside of the ice and coal shed. Before the depression the coal man had carried his ice and coal in a wagon drawn by a horse. But when the depression came he had to sell his horse because he was not able to feed it and had pushed his ice and coal and wood around in a hand push cart. He left the wagon standing outside because he had no other place to put it.

George Sampson skated around awhile, slid up and down the side alley, at the same time keeping an eye on Sam Smith's house waiting and watching for Sam to come out and go to the store.

The coal and ice shed was located in the middle of the block on the west side of Jones Avenue, a cross street. Sam Smith lived on the east side of

Jones Avenue, almost opposite the coal and ice shed but a little to the right. The school was located on Elm Avenue, the first intersecting street left of the coal and ice shed. Next door to the coal and ice shed, on the left, was a side alley. Left of the alley was a small church located in what had once been a store. The first intersecting street to the right of the coal and ice shed was Maple Street. At the corner of Maple and Jones Streets on the same side of the street with Sam Smith's house was the grocery store to which Sam went every evening after school.

Sam Smith lived in a small one-story and a half cottage with a small front yard and a large side yard. The back rooms of the house projected out into the side yard thereby forming a kind of elongated corner.

Although snow covered the ground the weather was not extremely cold and George Sampson kept skating up and down the side alley where the snow was somewhat trampled down. As he rollicked he kept watching Sam Smith's house to see him when he came out to go to the store. He made up several snow balls in anticipation of Sam's appearance.

After a while Sam Smith came around the side yard and out of the front gate and proceeded on his way to the store.

George Sampson hid around the corner of the side alley with the snow balls in readiness. Sam Smith took a few leisurely slides in the direction of the store. When Sam got within throwing distance George Sampson grabbed a snow ball, sailed it across the street at him and ducked back around the corner of the side alley. Sam Smith turned all around to see where the snow ball came from. At first he saw no one.

George Sampson chuckled to himself, threw another snow ball and ducked back around the side of the alley. Sam Smith spied George Sampson around the corner of the side alley and threw a snow ball at him. George Sampson dodged behind the wagon in front of the coal and ice shed and made ready three snow balls. Sam Smith with a snowball in each hand looked all around to see where George Sampson had escaped to. George Sampson was nowhere in sight. So Sam dropped the snow balls and trotted on to the store, looking cautiously back over his shoulder as he went. George Sampson crouched behind the wagon with three snow balls in readiness watching and waiting for Sam's return.

He was so busy watching for Sam that he did not see the coal man coming down Elm Street with the push cart full of empty baskets to be filled and taken to the customers before supper time. As Sam was on his way back from the store George Sampson sailed a snow ball at him and then ducked down behind the wagon. Sam turned all around in an attempt to locate George Sampson. George Sampson, from his point of vantage behind the wagon, chuckled to himself and took another snow ball, hopped up and sailed it at Sam and ducked down again, but not quickly enough. In his haste he accidently knocked over one of the coal man's baskets of wood.

Sam Smith spied George Sampson, ran and sailed a snow ball at him and then ran back in the yard and hid around the corner of the house.

Just as Sam threw the snow ball the coal man turned the corner and proceeded down Jones Street enroute to his coal shed. The snow ball directed at George Sampson whizzed past the coal man and caused him to step back.

Meanwhile George Sampson reached down for the other snow ball.

The coal man looked to see where the snow ball had come from but saw no one. So he continued on toward his coal and ice shed still on the guard for snow balls. As he was about to turn down the side alley into his coal shed he saw his basket of wood turned over and stooped to pick it up. As he was picking up the basket of wood George Sampson rose up with the snow ball in his hand. He intended to throw it at Sam who was peeping from behind the corner of his house. The coal man spied George Sampson and his temper rose. All the harm that George Sampson had ever done loomed up before him. The coal man's brother came out to see what was going on and took in the situation at a glance.

"Oh there he is," muttered the coal man, "an' throwin' snow balls at me afta scratchin' on my slate an' turnin' ova my baskets an' mockin' me but I'll git him all right 'nough—I'll git him."

With that he started stealthily toward George Sampson. George Sampson felt the presence of some one, turned around, saw the coal man coming toward him with danger in his eye; sensed the situation, dropped the snow ball, and lit out for home with the coal man close behind him.

"Ketch 'im an' beat 'im good!" yelled the coal man's brother, "an' gib 'im one f'me."

The coal man was running so fast that he did not have the breathe to answer. Several passersby turned and stared trying to see exactly what was going on.

Two of George Sampson's pals coming down the street spied George Sampson in the lead and the coal man close behind. They took in the situation at a glance and yelled, "Run George Sampson, run!"

Sam Smith looked on from a safe distance and laughed uproariously.

When George Sampson had sped about two blocks he looked back and attempted to catch his breathe. He saw the coal man gaining on him. He cut across the lots, leaped over the back fence and flew into the kitchen door like the traditional cyclone.

"What's th' matter, George Sampson?" asked Lottie in alarm, "didn't you git th' boy?"

THE TEACHER'S PICTURE

The children filed in from the noon intermission two by two. Grouch and gloom were registered on George Sampson's face. He had been compelled to stay in one half hour at noon and finish his arithmetic which he had neglected to work at the regular period.

Miss Smith was standing talking to Mrs. Nelson, a parent, who had come over to see about her boy's work and attendance.

"Now children," cautioned Miss Smith shaking her finger impressively at the group as they passed her in the hall, "be sure an' let me find everyone in his seat an' busy. You'll find your work on the board."

Miss Smith believed in having the work on the board when the children came in so that they would lose no time in getting down to business and have less time to get into mischief.

The children placed their wraps in the cloakroom, some with more orderliness than others. George Sampson reluctantly placed his cap on his hook, satisfied himself by pulling a girl's hair and swung down the aisle, balancing himself on the desks and swinging himself up in the air until he reached his seat. He knew from past experience that it was best to be found in his own seat. He had been found out of his seat several times and as a result had been kept in. And he hated staying in.

The children found their seats amid a general buzzing, turning and whispering. They took out their notebooks and went about the work on the board.

The work on the board consisted of a number of key signatures which the children were to copy into their music notebooks.

George Sampson, again, wrote his name on the back of the notebook, then pushed it aside, looked toward the door to see if the teacher were coming and, seeing that the "coast was clear" pulled a finger-printed piece of manila paper from his pocket and turned around confidentially to John, laid the piece of paper on his desk saying, "Looka here don that look lak hu?" The "hu" referred to Miss Smith.

John looked up from his work, took the picture, looked at it and said, "Boy that looks jis lak hu —what'y gonna do with it—put it on hu desk before she comes in why dontchy? Write hu name under it an' see what she says."

"No boy," explained George Sampson, "I ain't gonna put it on hu desk 'cause she might git it mixed up with them otha papers an' not see it. I'm gonna draw it right here on th' board great big soon's I git a chance an' put hu name under it an' make hu good an' mad 'cause she come keepin' me in at noon an' I didn't git to play ball time I got through eatin' my lunch. But don tell hu who drawed it y'hear," cautioned George Sampson.

"You oughta say 'drew,'" corrected John conscious of the language lesson of a few days before.

"Well anyway," went on George Sampson passing off the correction lightly, "don tell hu nuthin'."

"No boy," promised John faithfully, "I cross my heart an' hope to die. Why dontchy draw it now before she gits in?"

"That's right!" ejaculated George Sampson. "Here's a piece of chalk." He reached over to the side blackboard panel between the windows and took off a piece of chalk. . . . The last bell ain't rung yet," he continued, "an' she's talkin' to that lady—maybe I could git it done before she gits in here."

"Say gets," recommended Helen Jenkins looking up airily from her work.

"Oh shut up ole girl," retorted George Sampson, "it don make no difference what I say long as I say it."

Helen turned up her nose contemptuously and went on with her work.

George Sampson looked toward the door and seeing the way clear reached over to the side blackboard panel and began to draw. Two or three of the children looked up with interest glad to have a diversion. John, the boy behind George Sampson, kept one eye on George Sampson and one eye on the door. "Go 'head boy," he whispered, "an' I'll tell'y whin she's comin'.'"

George Sampson made a few more strokes. Several children looked on.

"You betta stop that," advised Helen Jenkins, "an' go on with your work before you make some more fat zeros."

Several children laughed.

George Sampson turned up his nose, then made a few more strokes.

A shadow appeared across the door.

"Watch out boy, 'rase it, 'rase it, here she come, here she come," cautioned John.

George Sampson scrambled for an eraser, erased the drawing, placed the chalk back on the board, moved back over into his seat and assumed an innocent look.

Miss Smith came in. The children went on with the work in their notebooks.

George Sampson pretended to be deeply interested in his work but his mind was on other things.

"Now let me see who can pass the language books real quickly?" asked Miss Smith.

George Sampson promptly raised his hand with the exclamation, "Lemme pass 'em."

"No George Sampson," replied Miss Smith, "you remember when you passed books this morning you cracked a boy on the head. Now Sam you pass the books an' Thelma you pass the paper."

Sam Smith rose with dignity and took the keys and went to the book-case. Sam had the happy faculty of moving around the room without creating any disturbance. Each child had his name in a book and was responsible for that particular book. The books were arranged in the case according to the way the children were seated in rows. Thelma moved around lightly and passed a sheet of lined manila paper to each child.

After the language books and the paper were duly passed, the teacher explained to the children that they were to take the Exercise beginning on page 147, copy the sentences, place the correct word where the blank was and underline the word used.

William wrote the first sentence on the board: "The children are playing."

"That is correct," approved the teacher. "Now what shall we put in the second blank 'The child ——playing?' "

"Is," answered the children in concert.

"That's right," replied the teacher as she looked around to see if all the children were paying attention. She discovered George Sampson half way out of his seat reaching over marking on the blackboard panel.

"George Sampson," commanded Miss Smith, "get back over in your seat an' stop marking on that board. Now what did I say do?"

George Sampson "hemmed and hawed" and looked around to see if someone would assist him. Receiving no help he finally said reluctantly, "You say write some sentences."

"Is that so—what kind of sentences?" questioned the teacher further.

"Jis sentences," grumbled George Sampson.

"Um-hum," disapproved the teacher. "Helen tell him what I said do."

Helen rose airily, looked squarely at George Sampson and stated what was to be done. George Sampson looked sheepish.

"Now children," went on Miss Smith, "you'll have half an' hour to finish your work. Mary write the assignment on the front board. Now children do your best writing an' try to have 100 so that your paper can go on the bulletin board."

Then she sat down to check the attendance and to write out the transfer cards for four children who were to be transferred to another school; and to complete the records which went along with these transfers.

When a child was transferred to another school four records had to be made out. Before preparing the transfer records Miss Smith took out her roll book and began to check the attendance.

"Where is Marjorie?" asked Miss Smith, looking up from the roll book.

"She's absent," answered two or three children near the teacher's desk.

"Goody," murmured George Sampson as he slipped a piece of chalk from the board and put it into his desk.

As Miss Smith continued to mark the roll book a stirring occurred over by the door. The children near the door were looking toward the door and moving around in their seats. Evidently someone outside the door was trying to get attention but did not want to come in. Miss Smith looked up to see what was going on. Mary, a stout, serious-minded girl in the front seat raised her hand and said, "Miss Smith, Sallie's mother wants to see you. She's outside the door."

The children looked toward the door and some of them looked at Sallie. George Sampson looked at Sallie and went through the mouth motions of saying, "Oh-oh-oh."

Miss Smith placed the book mark in her roll book, closed it and cautioned the children to go on with their work while she was out and not to have any disorder or talking.

The children worked quietly for a few minutes. George Sampson looked around to see what the prospects of having a good time were. Seeing all the children busy at work and no immediate prospects of a good time in sight he resumed his work but continued fidgeting and fuming around. The children paid little attention to him as they wished to have their papers completed in time and a good mark on them.

George Sampson continued to squirm and whisper around but failed to attract attention. Finally he announced defiantly, "I'm gonna draw hu pitcha an' nobodee betta not tell hu I drawed it neitha—'cause if they do I'll bust 'em in th' nose."

He turned half way around, slipped the chalk out of his desk and kept one eye on the door as he reached over to the side board panel and began to sketch, whispering to John, "Looka here boy I'm gonna draw it now sho 'nough."

John said, "Boy you betta watch out she'll get you."

The children looked up from their work with interest. Some giggled and said, "You betta not do that. I bet she'll get you. She'll be good an' mad."

Some of the little girls threatened to tell the teacher.

"Jis tell hu an' see what you git," retorted George Sampson shaking his fist in a menacing manner. "Jis tell hu if you wanna."

He grasped the chalk and with one eye on the door he made a circle or what he termed a circle. This circle represented the face. Then he made a straight line for the part in the hair and put the smooth black hair on each side of the part. Lastly he added a pair of goggle glasses. Then he printed under it "Mis Smith."

The children looked up and commented.

Some said, "Boy you betta 'rase it."

Others said, "Boy she's gonna get you—oh boy, I betchu she'll be mad."

"Well don tell hu nuthin'," commanded George

Sampson to all whom it may have concerned, "or I'll bust you in th' nose."

He was putting a few finishing touches on the picture when Miss Smith finished her conversation with Sallie's mother and moved toward the door.

William, a long, lanky boy near the door, saw the teacher's shadow on the wall and sounded the warning, "Sh-sh here she come."

George Sampson jumped back over into his seat, grabbed his pencil and began writing his sentences with a vengeance.

The door opened. Miss Smith came in. The children pretended to be hard at work.

Miss Smith walked over to the desk, took a seat, looked around, had some children pick up the paper from the floor beside their seats and then continued marking the roll book.

The children watched with one eye on their work and one eye on the teacher to see what she was going to do about the picture. Miss Smith finished marking the roll book and serenely went about writing out the transfer and record cards. Once she looked up and asked, "How many have finished?"

No hands were raised.

"You have about ten minutes more," advised the teacher evidently taking no notice of the picture.

The children were puzzled. Some looked at Miss Smith and then at the picture in an attempt to draw Miss Smith's attention to the picture. Some of the little girls tried to catch Miss Smith's eye and pointed to the picture and then to George Sampson indicating that George Sampson was responsible for the picture. Miss Smith looked vacantly at them and then went back to writing out the transfer records. At intervals she looked around to see if the children were doing their work.

The children cast sly looks at each other and at the picture and smiled and looked at the teacher to see what she was going to say. Miss Smith continued to write out the transfer records.

The teacher completed the transfer records. George Sampson watched and wondered and puzzled. Finally he wrote a note saying, "I wonder can she see good" and turned around and slipped it to John. The other children kept watching and waiting to see what was going to happen and searching each other's faces for an explanation. As nothing seemed likely to happen they sighed and settled back to work.

George Sampson, however, was not able to settle. He continued to fumble around, wrote a sentence, looked out of the window, wrote another sentence, looked around at the picture and then at the children near him and ducked his head down and laughed. He looked about him again to see what the children were doing and what the teacher was doing. Nobody paid any attention to him as the children had just about given up hope of having some fun from the picture. He ducked his head down again and called, "Z-Z-Z," to the children around him louder than he thought and pointed to the picture.

The children looked up all attention. The teacher raised her head slowly, looked sternly at George Sampson and directly at and through the picture and demanded severely of George Sampson, "Have you finished your work or do you wish to finish after school?"

The children looked with puzzled expressions on their faces. They looked from the picture to the teacher and to George Sampson and back again.

George Sampson with a sigh of chagrin and disappointment settled down to work.

GEORGE SAMPSON SENDS A
VALENTINE

Monday noon, the first day in February. Snow covered the ground and the snow was still falling. The children did not go out to play at the noon intermission because the weather was cold, the snow falling, and a sharp wind blowing.

As the school had no playroom the children had to spend their noon hour in their own rooms. A number of schools had gymnasiums or playrooms in the basement where Physical Training was carried on and where the children played on inclement days. Sometimes if the playrooms were large enough assembly exercises were held in them. In schools having no gymnasiums or playrooms the children spent their extra time on inclement days in the class-room. Often the noon intermission was shortened and school was dismissed at 3:00 instead of 3:30. Those children who went home to lunch returned to their rooms as soon as they reached school. Those who brought their lunches remained in the room.

In order to furnish the children with a little recreation, Miss Smith allowed them to sit together after they had eaten their lunches and play tick-tack-toe or talk quietly. They were also allowed to go to the blackboard and write and talk as long as they were orderly and did not run around the room. If they became too noisy or disorderly the teacher instructed them to go to their own seats.

George Sampson had brought his lunch, two ham sandwiches and a piece of cake, and eaten it in a hurry. He would like to have run around the room or engaged in a wrestling bout but he thought best not to do so. So he contented himself by getting Thomas Brown up to the board to play tick-tack-toe. As they were playing Robert Williams came in from lunch and stood and looked at the game awhile, then drew a frilly valentine on the board.

Robert Williams was an excellent art scholar and delighted in drawing.

George Sampson and Thomas Brown stopped playing tick-tack-toe to admire the valentine and Robert Williams said, "We're gonna make valentines in drawing pretty soon, ain't we?"

"Yeh, we ought to be startin' pretty soon," replied George Sampson and Thomas.

Then the conversation drifted. Thomas looked out of the window and exclaimed, "Oh boy! Look how it's snowin'. I'm gonna get my sled out this evenin'. I'm gonna clean snow an' make some money too an' put it in my bank."

"I don lak to clean snow," complained George Sampson, "I sho don lak to."

As they were standing at the blackboard they overheard a group of little girls in the B. Class,

Marjorie, Helen Jenkins, Sophie Campbell and Thelma Wells discussing promotion day and their respective possibilities of being "put up."

Marjorie and Helen Jenkins were sitting in the seat together. Sophie and Thelma were seated in front of them and were turning around talking. Carrie James, a timid little girl, was standing near.

"Do you think she's gonna put you up?" asked Sophie of Thelma. The "she" referred to Miss Smith.

"Yes I think she's gonna put me up," replied Thelma because I didn't have any 4's or 5's on my report card, only 2's and 3's."

"Well I had one 4 on my card so I oughta get put up," said Sophie.

"Well she gimme two 4's but she ain't gimme no 5's," put in Carrie James.

"Puttin' up day's Friday," mused Marjorie and we get our report cards, too. I think I'll get put up 'cause I got all 2's on my card."

Every five weeks the children received report cards which were to be taken home, signed by the parent and returned. The cards were marked in terms of numbers, 1,2,3,4,5; meaning namely; excellent, good, fair, poor and failing. The children were marked in their scholarship in various subjects and also in the various qualities of character. There was also a place on the card for remarks to be written by the teacher.

George Sampson and his friends overheard the

discussion of the little girls and being likewise interested in promotion day began to discuss their respective possibilities of being, "put up."

"Boy puttin' up day's Friday, ain't it?" said Thomas Brown.

"Sure is," answered Robert Williams," 'cause Thursdee's the graduatin' exercises. My brotha's gonna graduate an' go to high school. He's in No. 1, A. Class. Miss Smith said I can go to th' exercises."

"Wonder is she gonna put me up in th' A. Class," worried Jesse Redd, who had just come back from lunch and was standing listening to the conversation.

"Well she oughta put me up," asserted Thomas Brown 'cause I got all 3's on my card. I didn't git no 4's."

"I just had one 4 on my card," put in Jesse. "I didn't have no 5's. So I think I oughta get put up."

"I jus had one 4 on my card," stated Robert Williams, "so I think she oughta put me in th' A. Class. I betchu she'll put Marjorie up in the A. Class 'cause she likes Marjorie."

"Sure but Marjorie do good work though," observed Thomas Brown. "You know she go by yo work an' not by how much she laks you."

Poor George Sampson was listening, turning the situation over in his mind and feeling much discouraged as he feared that his possibilities for being put up were very slim. He remembered that his report card had been everything but presentable and that the teacher had written under Remarks, "Can do, but wastes time." He would have preferred to remain silent but as all the others had spoken he felt duty bound to speak so he said, "Well she gimme a whole lotta 4's an' 5's 'cause she don lak me an' I bet she ain't gonna put me up neitha. My Mamma know she don lak me."

"Yeah but you know you don work all th' time George Sampson," advised Thomas Brown, "an' a lotta times you come late. Y'got t'work every day. Y'can't jus work one day and rest an' fool around two or three days."

"I know that but she wouldn't gimme nuthin' if I did work," persisted George Sampson, " 'cause she jis don lak me nohow,"

"Yeah but you oughta do some work an' see," insisted Thomas.

At this moment the bell rang and the children went to their own seats to go about the afternoon's work. The children who had been writing on the board erased their work and put the chalk and erasers back in place. Those children who had been sitting in other seats talking looked to see that they left no trash or paper on the floor.

George Sampson tried to concentrate on the afternoon's work in view of the fact that promotion day was near. But try as he would he could not get his mind off the 4's and 5's and "side remarks" that the teacher had written on his report card. The conviction in his mind that the teacher did not like him and so gave him bad marks on his report card haunted him. Then the thought struck him that maybe if he could do something to overcome the teacher's dislike for him she might relent and promote him. He racked his brain for a solution; but rack his brain as he might he could not seem to find a suitable solution to the problem and promotion day was Friday.

He watched the snow as it piled up, but the snow brought no solution. Three o'clock came. The snow had stopped falling. School was dismissed and still the problem had not solved itself.

When George Sampson got down to the gate Lottie was there waiting for him.

"Snow sure is deep ain't it?" observed Lottie.

"Yes," answered George Sampson absently.

And as they trudged along he did not say any more. He was busy with his thoughts. They passed a number of store windows decorated with valentines of all kinds and sizes, big valentines, little valentines, lacy valentines and plain valentines. Lottie looked at them with eager eyes but George Sampson was too deep in his own thoughts to notice them.

Rosie Carter and her little sister came running by and said, "Oh ain't those pretty valentines."

"Yeh it'll soon be Valentine Day," exclaimed Lottie. "Look at all those pretty valentines. That lace one is so pretty. I wish'd I had it."

"Yeh it is pretty," agreed George Sampson

absently,—and then an idea struck him. He exclaimed enthusiastically, "I b'lieve I'll give that ole Miz Smith a valentine."

"How come?" asked Lottie in surprise, "I thought you didn't lak hu."

"I don," affirmed George Sampson emphatically, "an' she don lake me neitha an' I don think she's gonna put me up but maybe if I give hu a real pretty valentine she might feel good an' put me up. 'Cause she laks pretty pitchas an' things."

"That's right," agreed Lottie, "that sure is a good idea 'cause the laks pretty pictures and things don she? She's got a lotta pretty pictures on the wall an' flowers in th' windows, but them lacy valentines cost ten cents an' you ain't got ten cents is'y?"

"No," replied George Sampson, "but maybe I could git it somehow. Maybe I could do some work for somebodee or sompin' but what could I do?" He went on talking half to himself and half to Lottie. "I know," he flashed as they shuffled along in the snow. "I'll clean off snow for somebodee—a lotta peeple ain't got they sidewalks cleaned off yet."

"I thought you didn't lak to shovel off snow," said Lottie greatly surprised knowing what a struggle Granny always had to get George Sampson to clean off their sidewalk at home.

"I don," complained George Sampson, "but I gotta git put up somehow. Friday's puttin' up day an' I gotta work fast. I'll clean our snow off real quick," he ruminated, "an' then I'll ask Granny t'lemme go out an' clean snow so I kin git the valentine tomorrow, 'cause y'know Friday's puttin' up day. Now don't y'tell nobodee what I'm cleanin' this snow off for, not even Granny an' I'll give you a nickel if I makes two dimes."

"I ain't gonna tell nobody," promised Lottie, "I cross my heart."

As soon as they reached home George Sampson rushed in with enthusiasm and asked, "Granny kin I git th' spade and clean off our sidewalk an' then go an' clean snow for peeple before it gits dark so I kin hab a little sompin' extra to put in my bank?"

"Well, sho, George Sampson," replied Granny opening her eyes wide with surprise knowing how George Sampson had always hated to clean off snow, "but don you wanna eat yo dinna first?"

"No'am," declared George Sampson hastily, "I wanna get out before dark. I'll eat when I gits through. I'll clean ours off real quick. Where's th' spade?"

"Why it's out in th' coal shed," answered Granny hardly believing her own ears. "Wait I'll give'y th' key."

George Sampson took the key and went down the plank walk back to the coal shed, unfastened the padlock, opened the shed door, got the spade,

put the padlock back on and took the key back
to Granny.

"Now lissen George Sampson," cautioned
Granny, "don stay out too late an' keep on yo
gloves. Is'y got yo rubbers on? Now don git yo
feet cold. Here's a han'chief to tie up yo money
in so's yo won't lose it an' whin somebodee pays
you th' money be sho an' say, 'Thank you.' "

"Yessum," answered George Sampson as he put
the handkerchief in his pocket and started out
spade in hand. He walked over two blocks, crossed
the street and decided to start. The first house
that looked promising was a little cottage with an
iron fence, an iron gate and a small front yard.
He opened the gate, went in and timidly knocked
at the door.

A thin lady with a gingham apron on opened the
door and peeped out.

"Do you want somebodee to clean off yo snow
lady?" asked George Sampson timidly.

"Why no son, my husband'll clean it off when
he comes home," explained the lady kindly, "maybe the lady next door wants hers cleaned off."

"Yessum," mumbled George Sampson backing
down the steps and out of the gate.

The house next door was a tall frame which
set far back in the yard. The yard was shut in by
a picket fence with a picket gate which fastened
with a rope. George Sampson opened the gate
and walked down the plank walk to the house.
A stout girl came to the door in response to George

Sampson's knock and said that her brother would clean off the snow when he came home.

George Sampson was much discouraged. He went slowly out of the gate and over to a little frame house across the street and tried again.

A motherly old lady with gray hair and spectacles came to the door and said, "Yes I would like to get my snow cleaned off. How much will you charge?"

George Sampson replied that he would charge fifteen cents.

"Alright," agreed the lady, "go ahead and clean it."

George Sampson brightened up with enthusiasm. He "put his best foot forward." In spite of his cold hands he scraped and shoveled and threw snow in four different directions until the sidewalk was cleared of every trace of snow.

As he was scraping and shoveling the lady next door raised the window, called out and asked George Sampson how much he charged to clean snow.

George Sampson answered, "Fifteen cents."

"Alright," said the lady, "I would like for you to clean mine off when you get through."

George Sampson completed his work in a creditable manner which would certainly have surprised Granny and his mother and Lottie to say nothing of Miss Smith. The motherly old lady had him come in and warm his hands at the kitchen stove while she got the money.

George Sampson thanked the lady as Granny had instructed him, tied the fifteen cents in the corner of his handkerchief, stuffed the handkerchief in his pocket and hurried over to the house next door. He cleaned the second sidewalk doggedly, received his fifteen cents, said, "Thank you," tied the fifteen cents up in the opposite corner of his handkerchief and trudged home jubilant in spirits in spite of his cold hands and feet.

Mrs. Brite arrived home from work shortly before George Sampson returned home from cleaning snow.

"Where is George Sampson?" asked his mother.

Granny and Lottie told her that he was out cleaning off snow.

Mrs. Brite was duly surprised and exclaimed, "Out cleanin' snow! Land sakes alive! What's gonna happen!"

Just at that moment George Sampson came in shivering with cold but jubilant with thirty cents in his pocket.

"How much did y'make?" asked Lottie and Granny together.

"I made thirty cents," enthused George Sampson getting up to the kitchen stove to warm his hands. "I shoveled snow f'two ladies an' each one gimme fifteen cents."

"Well that sho is fine," commended Granny and his mother, "what'y gonna do wid it?"

"I'm gonna put fifteen cents in my bank an'

take ten cents to school to buy sompin' an' here's
a nickel f'you Lottie."

"My how nice," approved Mrs. Brite and
Granny. "Did y'say, 'Thank you' Lottie?"

"Yes'm," replied Lottie.

"Well now," instructed Granny, "warm yo'self
good George Sampson an' then set down an' eat yo
dinna."

So George Sampson warmed himself by the
stove and ate his dinner in a highly excited state.

The next morning the weather was a trifle
warmer but the snow was still on the ground.
George Sampson got up earlier than usual and was
ready for school before Lottie. Lottie, sensing
what was in George Sampson's mind hurried with
her preparations and they got away about ten
minutes earlier than usual and trudged through
the snow, lunches under arm.

"You gonna git th' valentine this morning?"
asked Lottie, "or you gonna wait till noon?"

"No I betta git it this morning 'cause I don
want all them otha chil'rin to know 'bout it," said
George Sampson. "It's early an' I wanta give it
to hu 'cause this is Tuesday an' puttin' up day's
Friday."

"Yeh that's right," agreed Lottie, "You betta
work fast."

So they trudged on through the snow until
they came to the little store where the valentines
were. They looked in the window and discussed

the valentines a minute before they went into the store.

"I think that one way up there is pretty." exclaimed Lottie.

"Yeh," said George Sampson thoughtfully, "that one ova there's pretty, too. Let's go in an' look at them good."

They went inside the store. The lady got out a box of valentines of every description. George Sampson and Lottie looked them over eagerly.

"This is a nice one," said Lottie picking out a frilly, lacy one with little hearts and cupids all over it. "One that stands up."

"Yeh that is a nice one," replied George Sampson and it says, 'For my Teacher.'"

"An' here's a nice verse about the teacher," observed Lottie, "yeh this is a fine one." She asked the lady to wrap it up real nice because it was for the teacher.

"Why sure," returned the lady. "I'll wrap it up real nice in this yellow paper an' tie it with a red string."

George Sampson asked Lottie to carry the valentine until they got to school. He did not want to make himself in any way conspicuous by carrying anything that looked like a present for the teacher. So Lottie took charge of the package. They reached school about 8:30.

The children were going to their regular rooms from the early room. The majority of the children had not yet arrived.

"Do you think I oughta write my name on it or not?" asked George Sampson.

"Yeh, I think so," advised Lottie, "so she'll be sure an' know you give it to hu. Come on in my room. Miss Wray won't care. I'll write on it with my red wax crayon."

Clara Smith and Minnie May, both in Lottie's room and good friends of hers were going down the hall as she and George Sampson were arriving. Lottie's room was the highest room on the first floor. Richard Jones, Rosie Carter and her little sister, Millie, were already in the room when Lottie and George Sampson reached the door. Sara Stone, a little girl who was not so friendly to Lottie, was coming in the door as Lottie and George Sampson were standing outside the door, preparatory to going in. Sara made a face at Lottie and Lottie "returned the compliment."

So they took the package into Lottie's room and Lottie wrote on it with red crayon, "To Miss Smith from George Sampson. Happy Valentine." Then she gave the package to George Sampson.

George Sampson felt very awkward with the package in his possession. He kept turning over in his mind how he should present the package and whether or not he should say, "Happy Valentine." Luckily when he reached his room on the second floor he found Miss Smith standing outside of the door, in the hall looking out of the window at the snow. She looked surprised to see George

Sampson at school so early and said, "Good morning."

"Good mornin'," replied George Sampson and stepped forward and presented the package.

Miss Smith read the note on the outside, opened the package and exclaimed, "Oh what a pretty valentine! Is this for our drawing lesson?"

"No'am," answered George Sampson timidly, "it's for you."

"For me," exclaimed the teacher, "my how nice! Well I certainly appreciate it." And she went into the room and stood it up on her desk in a very conspicuous place.

George Sampson was highly elated and thought surely this would accomplish the purpose and get him "put up." He went about his school work with great zest.

The snow was still on the ground and the weather was growing colder. The children had indoor recess and also indoor noon. School was dismissed at 3:00.

Lottie did not see George Sampson again until school had been dismissed. As soon as she saw him she rushed up and inquired about the valentine. "Did you give hu th' valentine?" she asked with hurried curiosity. "How did she lak it?"

"She laked it fine," answered George Sampson. "She stood it right up on th' desk where everybodee could see it."

"Well then I guess she'll put you up," said Lottie. "I think I'm gonna get put up in th' A. Class."

"I hope she'll put me up," worried George Sampson. "Friday's puttin' up day. She sho did lak th' valentine. That oughta git me sompin'."

The teachers had made triplicate lists of the children who were to be promoted and those who were not. Two of these lists were sent to the principal. One was kept by the original teacher. One the principal gave to the new teacher to whom the children were sent.

The graduating exercises were scheduled for 10:30 A.M., Thursday. The A. Class of Room I was to graduate. This would cause a promotion throughout the school. Those children who were in the A. Classes of each room and who had finished their work satisfactorily would be promoted to the next room. Those in the B. Classes who had finished their work satisfactorily would be promoted to the A. Class of the room in which they were.

Sometimes all of the pupils of Room I were graduated. This caused a general moving up of the rooms throughout the school. In June the whole of Room I was to be graduated.

Wednesday passed uneventfully.

Thursday morning the children were working diligently anticipating promotion day. Just before the exercises the graduates, all bedecked in their graduating costumes and colors, marched through each room so that all of the children would have an opportunity to see them and be inspired to work hard and graduate. The boys marched erect in their dark suits. The girls were self-conscious in their white dresses and hair ribbons. The teachers and children clapped as they paraded in and out. Two girls, whose sisters were graduating, also had special permission to go to the exercises. As George Sampson gazed wide-eyed at the graduates he was struck with a sudden spark of inspiration to work hard and graduate if for no other reason than to get all dressed up and march around the rooms on graduating day.

Marjorie was in ecstacies as the graduates marched through and so enthusiastic that she could hardly stay in her seat.

"Tomorrow's putting up day isn't it?" exclaimed Marjorie.

"Yes," answered Miss Smith, "tomorrow is promotion day."

"I hope I get put in th' A. Class," said Marjorie.

"I hope so," replied Miss Smith.

George Sampson looked and listened hoping that the valentine would have the desired effect.

All that afternoon he gave strict attention to business.

The next day was Friday, the long anticipated "putting up day." Usually promotions were made in the afternoon as the teachers had several final reports to get out in the morning. The children worked with unusual diligence that morning. Children who had lazied along all the term were struck with a sudden desire to work.

School was to dismiss at 3:00. The recess and noon periods had been cut short. About 1:45 the principal took the lists, went to Room I and began to promote the children. In due time the principal reached Miss Smith's room and read the names of the children who were to be promoted to the room above. All of the A. Class were promoted except four children. Two had been absent on account of illness. The other two had not done any work until the day before promotion day. The children who were going to the next room got their wraps and personal belongings and went with the principal. Each child had his report card and each child carried his large attendance card and small attendance card to the next teacher.

Then Miss Smith called the names of the children in the B. Class who were promoted to the A. Class. One name was called and then another, Marjorie, Thelma, Thomas, Robert and on down the list. George Sampson kept straining his ears to hear his name but no "George Sampson." Those children whose names were called moved over on the A. Class side. George Sampson still looked and listened. The teacher folded up the list and put it away. Still no mention was made of George Sampson's name.

He and three others were left sitting on the B. Class side where they had been sitting since September. The principal came in and brought the children from the room below. They took seats all around George Sampson while the tears trickled down his cheeks.

Shortly the bell rang for dismissal. George Sampson got in the line with a heavy heart and a feeling of indignation at having wasted his labor and his beautiful valentine.

The lines passed out. Lottie was waiting at the gate for George Sampson and said gleefully, "I got put up in th' A. Class, did you?"

Poor George Sampson wept afresh and said, "No she ain't put me up nowhere an' afta I nearly worked myself to death to get that valentine for hu."

GEORGE SAMPSON'S LITTLE SISTER

Friday morning.—Early Spring. The season was changing from winter to spring and a chill was still in the air. Lottie's teacher, Miss Wray, was suffering from an earache that morning and was not able to assume her duties at school.

When George Sampson and Lottie reached school the early room had been dismissed. Lottie said, "I'm going in my room an' put my things up an' then go on th' playground. Come on in my room with me, George Sampson."

When they reached Lottie's room the children were moving around restlessly. No teacher was in sight. Some of the children were in their own seats, working, some were walking around talking and socializing with others.

Rosie Carter had brought her little sister, Millie, to the room with her. Millie had her doll. All the kindergarten children had been instructed to bring toys that day. A number of little girls crowded around Millie, exclaiming, "Ain't she cute," and looking at the doll and listening to it say, "Ma-ma."

When George Sampson saw no teacher in sight and a general moving around going on he decided the opportunity was at hand to have some fun. So he pulled Millie's doll baby's hair, called it a hard head baby and ran as Rosie hit at him.

As he went down the aisle he hit Richard Jones on the head, grabbed his hat and ran on down the aisle. Richard ran him out of the room and down the hall and retrieved his hat. Miss Morgan, the teacher in the next room, heard the commotion and went to investigate. She got the children seated and gave them some work to do. George Sampson left the scene when he saw no more fun in sight and went on outdoors. Shortly Miss Wray's mother telephoned and said that Miss Wray was ill and would not come to school that day.

The apprentice teacher, Miss Ross, came in and took charge of the room until such time as the substitute teacher would arrive.

The 9 o'clock bell rang. The principal came in and told the children that Miss Wray was ill and would not be able to come to school that day. Lottie, seeing a good time in sight, but with no ill wishes for the teacher, immediately began to clap.

"Why Lottie," disapproved the principal, "I'm surprised at you clapping when the teacher is ill. I'm sure the teacher wouldn't clap if you were ill. I think you should be sorry your teacher is ill."

Some of the other children nodded their heads in agreement and Lottie looked very much ashamed. In about one half an hour the substitute teacher arrived, a stout little teacher with short bobbed hair, whose name was Miss Jones. She wrote her name on the board in large script.

The children looked the teacher over and tried to approximate how much fun they could have. They were restless and talkative. Some took advantage of the occasion to throw a little chalk, while some hummed to themselves, others drew pictures of various things including the teacher. Others, to vary the monotony poked their neighbors with pencils. In short, "a good time was had by all." The principal came in once or twice and things quieted down for a few minutes and then resumed after the principal went out.

Monday morning Miss Wray returned and asked how everybody had fared in her absence and what the substitute teacher's name was. The children told her that the substitute teacher's name was Miss Jones and that some of the children "cut up" and talked and sang. Then Sara Stone raised her hand and airily and conscientiously told Miss Wray that, "When th' principal came in an' said that, you was sick an' couldn't come to school, Lottie clapped."

"Sho did," chimed in several other children.

The teacher looked at Lottie for several seconds and then asked in an injured tone, "What kind of a creature are you to clap when your teacher is ill? Just what kind of a creature are you anyway? When I was a little girl I was always sorry when my teacher was ill. I don't know what kind of a creature you can be."

A couple of children laughed and said, "Creeper, creeper, creeper—a creeper's a bug," and pointed to Lottie.

A little later a boy went to the waste can and as he passed by Lottie's seat whispered, "Hello creeper—a creeper's a bug, don't bite me."

Lottie looked very much chagrined.

When the lines went out at recess a number of children ran up to Lottie and asked her what kind of a creeper she was and ran. Then five or six children jumped up and down around Lottie and shouted, "Creeper, creeper, creeper, a creeper's a bug. She creeps over everything. Run! She might creep on you. She might bite you!"

Lottie began to cry and hit at the children. Richard Jones, who had gone over in the girl's yard to get his ball, saw the children dancing around Lottie and shouting, "Creeper, creeper, creeper," and saw Lottie hitting at them and and crying and rushed back and told George Sampson that his little sister was "just a crying."

"What's she cryin' 'bout?" demanded George Sampson excitedly.

Richard Jones replied that she was crying because the teacher called her names and the children were making fun of her.

"Well what names did she call hu!" questioned George Sampson.

"She called her a creeper or sompin," replied

Richard Jones, "an' the children's jis a'teasin' her."

"She ain't got no bizness callin' hu names an' I'm gonna tell Granny, too," exclaimed George Sampson indignantly.

George Sampson went over to the girl's fence and called Lottie. Lottie did not hear him at first. She was standing in the middle of a group of sympathetic listeners, weeping and telling her troubles. Minnie and Clara had their arms around her, others looked sympathetic and gave consoling advice saying, "She ain't got no bizness callin'y names. Y'tell yo gramma 'bout it."

Some little girls who were playing bean bag near the fence told Lottie that her brother wanted her. Lottie went over to the fence escorted by Clara and Minnie and followed by the sympathetic listeners.

Several boys came up to the fence and looked on wide-eyed.

"That ole teacher come callin' me names," sobbed Lottie. "She come callin' me a creeper an' all th' children was laughin' and makin fun a'me."

"Sho did," assented Minnie, Clara and the sympathetic listeners, "Sho did, she called hu a creeper an' all them chillun was just a laughin' an' making fun a hu an' saying a creeper's a bug."

"Well stop cryin'," counselled George Sampson, "an' tell me who th' chil'rin is that's makin' fun a you an' call you a bug an' I'll beat 'em up an' b'sides I'm gonna tell Granny when we gits home at noon an' she'll see how come she called'y them names. Now go wash yo face an' stop that cryin'.''

Clara and Minnie escorted Lottie to the basement to wash her face. Some of the sympathetic listeners followed. While they were in the basement the bell rang for the children to line up. Clara and Minnie attended Lottie to the line. Minnie was her partner and Clara stood behind her.

"Now stop lookin' lak you been cryin' an' be sure an' tell your gramma when you go home to lunch," they advised her.

The lines passed in and the children settled down to their geography work. The A. Class, Lottie's class, was studying the industries of the North Central States and the B. Class was studying the industries of the Pacific States. The children had about finished the industries and by way of review the teacher was having the classes dramatize one of the industries studied. The A. Class was preparing to dramatize the Wheat Industry of the North Central States while the B. Class was preparing to dramatize the Lumbering Industry of the Pacific States. The children were consulting supplementary books and text books for action pictures and information on the subjects. They were making notes in their geography notebooks. The next day the teacher planned to have them discuss the subject and work out class dramatizations in which all could participate. The children were very enthusiastic about the work and consulted the books diligently.

When the lines passed out at noon Lottie waited at the gate for George Sampson. Finally George Sampson's line came down. He peeked into Lottie's face to see if she were crying and cautioned her, "Now don start no mo cryin' but when y'gits home tell Granny what she called'y."

Lottie said very little as they walked along. George Sampson did not know what to say so he said nothing.

They cut across the lots and went into the kitchen door. Granny had the lunch all heated and setting on the stove; rice and chicken giblets. She also had a dish of chocolate pudding handy; another item left over from Sunday. The table was set and lunch was ready to be served.

As soon as Lottie got in the door she burst out crying while George Sampson stood and looked on sheepishly.

"What on earth is th' matta wid'y?" cried Granny in alarm. "Is'y sick or sompin?"

"That ole teecha called hu names," grumbled George Sampson, "an' all th' chil'rin was jis a'makin' fun a hu."

"What did she call hu?" queried Granny.

"Called hu a creeper or sompin," went on George Sampson.

"She called me a creeper," sobbed Lottie, "an' all th' children was just a'makin' fun a me."

"Well how come she called'y that?" questioned Granny, "what is she talkin' 'bout?"

"The chil'rin said a creeper's a bug," explained George Sampson, "an' all th' chil'rin was jis a'jumping up an' down sayin' she's a bug an' she'll bite you—she's a creeper, she'll creep on you."

"Why did th' teecha call'y that?" persisted Granny.

"Ain't no reason," sobbed Lottie, "just 'cause she don lake me."

"Well stop cryin' now," instructed Granny, "an' eat yo rice an' chicken giblets an' I'll go ova there an' see hu whin y'goes back. Who is she t'be callin' peeples chillun names? Now jis eat yo rice an' chicken giblets an' stop cryin'. Now wash yo face."

Lottie went to the kitchen sink, rinsed her face under the faucet and started crying again. Meanwhile George Sampson was seated at the oil-cloth covered kitchen table attacking the rice and chicken giblets and getting ready to tackle the chocolate pudding. Lottie sat down reluctantly at the table and minced along, ate a little of the rice and chicken giblets and then stopped.

"Now finish yo rice an' chicken giblets," bid Granny, "an eat yo puddin.'"

"I don want nuthin' more," wept Lottie.

George Sampson looked sympathetic but his eye was on the chocolate pudding.

After a few seconds he suggested, "Well then I'll eat yo puddin' if you don want it."

Lottie merely wept afresh and shook her head in assent.

"Well alright then take it then," said Granny to George Sampson. Then to Lottie, "Now stop that cryin' an' get th' basin from under the sink an' wash yo face good an' I'll go in th' middle room an' put on my otha dress an' shoes an' go back to school wid'y an' see why she's callin'y thim names."

So Granny got on her other dress and shoes and hat and coat and went on back to school with George Sampson and Lottie. The noon intermission was still in progress when Granny, Lottie, and George Sampson arrived. The children were playing around in the yard, chasing each other, eating ice-cream cones, pop-corn, peanuts, chocolate bars and other knickknacks. The boys were wrestling, running after each other and playing ball, some of the girls were walking around with their arms around each other while others were playing house. Several teachers were walking around the yard supervising the children.

Granny, Lottie and George Sampson entered the front gate and went up to the front door. Ordinarily the children did not go in at the front door until after the bell had rung. They went in at the side doors. The teacher in the front yard stepped up to see why Lottie, George Sampson and Granny were going in at the front door.

"This is my Gramma," said George Sampson

triumphantly, "she come ova to see 'bout sompin'.'"

"I see," said the teacher, "go right on in."

They went on in the front door and up to Miss Wray's room, No. 12.

As they opened the door they found Miss Wray sitting at the desk resting. Granny went in first with Lottie behind her. Lottie had an injured look on her face, and her mouth was stuck out. George Sampson followed close behind.

"How do you do?" said the teacher to Granny. "Is this Lottie's mother?"

No'am this is hu gramma," replied Granny.

"Oh yes, well I'm glad to see you," greeted Miss Wray, "how are you?"

"Very well, I thank you," answered Granny, "how's yo'self?"

"Well I'm much better," replied Miss Wray, "you know I was sick Friday an' had to stay home."

"I'm sorry y'been sick," said Granny sympathetically, "I hope y'fellin' betta."

"Yes I'm feeling all right now," said the teacher. "I had some trouble with my ear but it's getting all right. The doctor gave me some drops to put in it an' it's getting better."

"Well, that's good," said Granny.

A short silence followed. Lottie moved from one foot to another and looked injured. George Sampson kept looking at the teacher as though he were trying to read her mind.

Finally Granny cleared her throat and began,

"I jis come ova t'see 'bout Lottie. She come home this noon feelin' awful bad an' cryin' an' said you called hu a name or sompin' an' she felt awful bad 'bout it."

The teacher looked puzzled and said, "Why I haven't called her any name I don't know what she could be talking about I can't remember calling her anything."

"Yes'm you did," spoke up Lottie. "You called me a creeper."

"That's what all th' chil'rin said," put in George Sampson, "an' they said a creeper's a bug. They said you called hu a bug."

"Yessum," said Granny, "that's what she told me you called hu, a creeper; said what kind of a creeper was she anyhow an' all th' chillun made fun a hu an' said you called hu a bug an' jumped all up an' down an' teased hu."

"Oh," exclaimed the teacher, "I see what she's talking about.—Well you know I was sick Friday as I told you. Sick in bed an' couldn't come to school. So my mother called up an' reported that I was ill an' wouldn't be at school. So when the principal came in an' told the children I was ill an' couldn't come to school, Lottie clapped. An' when I came back the children told me about it an' I asked her what kind of a creature she was to clap when her teacher was ill. I should think she'd feel sorry for me, don't you? I didn't say anything about a creeper, I said a creature— c-r-e-a-t-u-r-e. Now a creature simply means some living thing. You an' I are creatures—we're all creatures. There's nothing for her to feel bad about. I can't see where she gets the bug part from. . . . Now I don't think it was very nice of her to clap when I was ill. Do you?"

The bell rang for the children to line up in the yard. Granny listened politely to the teacher, then answered, "No'am I don't think she oughta clap when you was sick an' a'course I wants hu to act nice an' so do hu mutha but please ma'am don't call hu no creeper no mo."

GEORGE SAMPSON AND THE GRASSHOPPER

"Oh look at the new teecha," exclaimed Thelma to Sophie as they arrived early Thursday morning and peeped in the door and espied a strange teacher at the blackboard, "I wonder where Miss Smith is an' who that new teecha is anyhow?"

The "new teacher," a substitute, well dressed, was writing on the board in a very business-like manner.

Thelma and Sophie hurried back downstairs and told Carrie and Marjorie and Sam that Miss Smith was absent and a new teacher was in the room, "A right classy looking teacher writing on the board."

The five rushed back upstairs, peeped in the door and then went in with a little more noise than necessary. The teacher turned around to see what was going on.

"Just stay downstairs until the bell rings for the lines to come in," ordered the teacher emphatically.

"Humph, hard-boiled," whispered Sam Smith, "telling somebody to go back downstairs. I wonder if we gonna have much fun? I betchu George Sampson's gonna have some fun all right enough."

The substitute teacher, Miss Wrice, was a very capable one, quite above the average. She had a very forcible personality, spoke clearly and decidedly, was well dressed and had quite an air of self-confidence. She wore a long-sleeved crepe dress of hyacinth blue. Her hair was shiny, waved and becomingly arranged. She knew the value of keeping the children busy with profitable work so as to hold their interest and not give them time to get into mischief. In her brief-case she carried a notebook of lesson outlines for the various grades, a box of colored blackboard chalk and some large, vividly colored pictures. She was especially good in blackboard sketching and in Science.

When the 8:45 bell rang for the lines to come in she had five examples in long division on the front board for the children to work and check, the paper distributed and a few pencils sharpened and ready to give out in case some child had no pencil and used this fact as an excuse to do no work and create disturbance.

When the lines came in the children gazed at the substitute teacher in silence, mentally sizing her up. They placed their wraps in the cloak-room, still gazing at the teacher and unconsciously surmising how much fun they could have.

"That sure is a pretty dress she got on," whispered Sophie to Carrie, "an' don't hu hair look nice."

"Sho do," whispered Carrie in reply.

The substitute teacher stood still until the children were all seated, waited a minute then said, "Good morning. My name is Miss Wrice." She turned around, wrote it in large letters on the board and drew two lines under it. Then she continued, "Miss Smith will not be here today. She is ill. You'll see your work on the board, five examples in long division to work and check. Now go right to work an' see if you can't make 100 because at 9 o'clock when the tardy bell rings I'm going to take up the papers and mark them and leave them right in the top drawer where Miss Smith can get them."

The children were awed by the forceful personality of the teacher. They listened attentively and started right off on their work.

George Sampson and a few of the other children had not yet arrived. The children worked diligently. In a few minutes Helen Jenkins came in carrying in her hand a bunch of sunflowers for the children to paint. She looked surprised when she saw another teacher at the desk in full charge. However she marched right up to the teacher's desk with the flowers and presented them to the substitute teacher saying, "I brought these flowers for us t'paint today."

"My how nice," exclaimed the teacher, "they certainly are pretty but I don't think we'll get to paint today since Miss Smith isn't here but you can put some water in this little blue vase an' maybe

they'll keep until tomorrow—anyhow they'll make
the room look prettier."

Helen took the little blue vase and half filled
it with water. Miss Wrice placed the sunflowers
in it and set it on the desk. Then she arranged the
other things on the desk. She placed a block of
manila paper on one side and the little compart-
ment tray with the rubber bands, thumb tacks and
pen points in it on the other side. She placed the
pencil box top turned upside down beside the box
of pencils. Then she put the drinking glass in
place.

About five minutes before 9 o'clock George
Sampson came sauntering in. He saw Miss Wrice
sitting up in he front of the room arranging the
things on the desk. He stood dumbfounded, on
seeing a new teacher and the children all busy at
work. In his opinion the proper thing to do was
to have a good time whenever the regular teacher
was absent and a substitute teacher in charge. He
thought to himself that if he had known that
Miss Smith wasn't gonna be at school he'd have
come earlier an' had some fun as the lines came
in. But he decided it wasn't too late to have some
fun and he was gonna have some fun anyhow as
soon as the opportunity presented itself. He
loitered to his seat and immediately turned around
and began whispering to the boy behind him and
looked back and tried to catch the eye of Thomas
and Robert.

Miss Wrice stood with her arms akimbo and

looked severely at George Sampson for a few seconds but said nothing. George Sampson became a little nervous and fidgety. Anybody looking directly at him always made him nervous. He grinned and squirmed and looked around to see how the other children were reacting to the situation. But when he saw that everyone was silent he continued to squirm and grin. He did not like to be stared at. The other children kept on with their arithmetic because they wanted to have 100.

"What is your name?" asked the teacher after staring at him a few more seconds.

"His name's George Sampson Brite," spoke up Thelma Wells from the other side of the room.

"Well I wish he'd govern himself accordingly," observed Miss Wrice,

The other children looked at George Sampson and grinned.

George Sampson assumed an injured look. He sensed that the odds were against him. He got out his wax crayon box slowly and stuck his pencil through the holes in the top of it. Then he opened it and took out his eraser and began to work the examples. He went on slowly with his work but determined in his mind to have some fun before the day was out regardless of the consequences. He was determined to take advantage of Miss Smith's absence because he said to himself, "It

wouldn't be no good for hu t'be absent if we
didn't hab no fun outa it."

Things progressed well enough for the first
hour and a half. Miss Wrice kept the children busy
and interested so that they had no time for foolishness. She had some large vividly colored pictures which she hung upon the wall in the front of
the room. Then she put the instructions upon the
front board. The children were to select a picture,
draw it with wax crayon and write in their own
words a story, not over eight sentences about the
picture. The teacher cautioned the children to
have a good beginning sentence and a good ending
sentence.

The children worked diligently on the stories
for some time. They delighted in drawing with
their colored crayons and in weaving stories about
the pictures.

When the allotted time was up the teacher had
the papers collected and the geography texts
passed out. The A. Class was studying Mexico
and the B. Class was studying Spain. Miss Wrice
explained to them that she wished each class to
make a product map of the country which they
had been studying. Then she explained the meaning of a product map. To make the point clearer
she took her green chalk and drew on the board
an outline map of the United States showing all
the states. She indicated the products of each
region by drawing pictures on the map of things
that grew in that region. She designated the corn

regions by drawing stalks of corn on the states
which produced corn; stacks of wheat on the wheat
producing states, bales of cotton on the cotton
states and piles of logs on the lumbering states.
She then explained to the children that they were
to do the same with the respective countries that
they were studying. The children were very much
interested, admired the teacher's drawing greatly
and went about their work with much zest.

George Sampson messed around with his
crayon box and kept sticking his pencil in the
holes he had punched in the top of it. The other
children were busy working trying to make a map
as pretty as the one the teacher had made. So
George Sampson seeing the other children busy
at work pretended to be doing some work. Bit
by bit he pieced together what he called an outline map of Spain. Every once in a while he looked
up to see how things in general were going, to
see if the time were ripe for him to have his fun.
Seeing that the opportunity did not present itself
he settled back to piecing the map together.

Recess came and George Sampson had not yet
had his fun. Some of the children were so interested in their work that they asked Miss Wrice
to let them stay in at recess and finish it. Miss
Wrice, however, told them that she thought it
best that they go out and get a little air and
exercise so they could work better after recess.
So the children left their materials where they
could get right to them when they returned, and

took their places in the line. The lines passed out very orderly in spite of George Sampson's efforts to have a little fun.

"That's a very good sub," remarked Miss Herman to Miss Green as they stood in the hall after the lines had passed down to recess. "She keeps the children busy and interested an' seems to have very good order. They say she's very intelligent an' progressive—goes to summer school and studies. I think she's interested in Art and Science."

"Yes, she's very good," replied Miss Green, "she's above the average. I wonder what that George Sampson's doing?"

"It's hard to tell," laughed Miss Herman. "I haven't heard anything of him yet but he's liable to start up before it's all over with."

"I wouldn't be surprised," smiled Miss Green.

Out in the girls' yard the substitute teacher was being discussed by the girls in Miss Smith's room and some of the girls in Miss Green's and Miss Herman's room.

"What is her name?" asked one.

"Is she easy?" asked another.

"Don't she look classy," put in a third.

"Yeh, she sure do look classy," agreed all the girls.

At the same time, in the boys' yard a similar discussion was going on with all the boys trying to talk at once.

"Did you all have a good time this morning,

I see old lady Smith ain't here?" they asked of George Sampson. "How is the new teacher? Is she hard-boiled?"

"She's a pain," complained George Sampson, "jis lak that ole lady Smith—tries t'be hard-boiled. We ain't had no fun yet but I'm gonna hab some fun all right 'nough I betchu. I sho am."

"Is'y sure 'nough boy?" inquired Thomas Brown, one of George Sampson's ardent admirers.

"Sho is," exclaimed George Sampson, "sho is."

"Here's a grasshopper," interrupted Robert Williams, coming up holding a large grasshopper in his hand. "I caught him with my hat."

"Oh boy, ain't he a big one," ejaculated George Sampson. "Look at him chewing tobacco. Listen boy, give him to me an' I'll let him loose an' hab some fun ofa that ole teecha what tries t'be so hard-boiled. I'll put him in my wax crayon box an' let him out all at once an' scare hu good."

Robert Williams was another ardent admirer of George Sampson.

"Will you sure 'nough let him loose?" asked Robert Williams increduously, gladly relinquishing the grasshopper at the prospect of so much fun.

"Sho boy," assured George Sampson, "I'm gonna put him in my crayon box an' let him out when she ain't lookin' an' don't y'all tell hu I done it neitha y'hear."

"No boy, I cross my heart," declared Robert Williams.

"Ain't y'scared boy?" queried Thomas Brown of George Sampson.

"No boy, no," boasted George Sampson.

"Kin he get air in your crayon box?" questioned Robert Williams fearing a "slip between the cup and the lip."

"Sho boy I got plenty holes in th' top a my crayon box," assured George Sampson.

At that moment the bell rang for the children to line up. George Sampson took his place on the line holding the grasshopper in his hand concealing it as much as possible but holding it so it could get air.

The lines came in very orderly, the children immediately took out their unfinished maps and resumed work on them.

Miss Wrice, however, had placed some new work on the board during the recess period. She told the children to finish the maps and then she would explain to them how to go about the new work. In about twenty minutes a number of the children had finished their maps. So Miss Wrice instructed all the children to lay aside the maps and give attention to the work on the board. She said that those who had not finished the maps would, no doubt, have time later on in the day to finish them.

The work on the board consisted of twenty-five words which had been taken from the reading lesson. The children were to look up the words in the dictionary, find the meanings and mark the words for pronunciation. Miss Wrice explained to the children exactly what they were to do.

All the children, except George Sampson, set to work immediately. Thomas Brown and Robert Williams went through the motions of work but their minds were on the grasshopper. The children worked diligently at their new work.

George Sampson was restless and fidgety. He pretended to be hard at work but at the same time he was watching and waiting for an opportunity to release the grasshopper. Thomas and Robert continued to go through the motions of work, with one eye on George Sampson and one eye on the teacher wondering when George Sampson was going to "turn the grasshopper loose." Miss Wrice sat at the desk marking the composition papers which the children had written. The other children were busy with their words. George Sampson watched the teacher as she marked the papers. He counted the three petals that fell from the sunflower onto the desk. Every now and then he looked through the holes in his wax crayon box to see if the grasshopper were O.K.

Ten more minutes passed in peace and quiet. Then a little girl raised her hand and asked how dotted a was pronounced. The teacher turned to the board and wrote the word "art" preparatory to explaining the pronunciation to the little girl.

As soon as the teacher turned her back Thomas and Robert raised up in their seats and began signalling to George Sampson. George Sampson needed no encouragement, however, because he sensed the psychological moment.

He pulled out his crayon box with a vengeance, dropping paper on the floor. Helen and Sophie looked over at him as he was dropping paper on the floor and frowned and pointed to the paper. Miss Smith had always cautioned them to keep paper off the floor. George Sampson paid no attention whatever to Helen and Sophie but gradually raised the top off of the crayon box. The grasshopper, glad to be free, jumped high into the air and lighted on Helen's desk. Helen squeaked and knocked it off. Miss Wrice turned around slowly to see what was taking place. The grasshopper took another jump and landed on Thelma Well's desk on the opposite side of the room. The children screamed with excitement. George Sampson and his pals chuckled with delight. Miss Wrice stood still and looked at the children with a fixed gaze. The children became a little more quiet wondering what the teacher would do. The grasshopper took a couple of short jumps and landed on the teacher's desk on one of the petals that had fallen from the sunflower. The children looked and laughed.

Miss Wrice eyed the grasshopper for a second and then skillfully took the pencil box top and brought it down over the grasshopper and confined him under it.

At this unexpected turn of affairs the children became very quiet and looked to see just what was going to happen next. Helen raised her hand and said conscientiously, "George Sampson did that, he had the grasshopper in his wax crayon box an' let him out."

"I ain't done nuthin'," ejaculated George Sampson chuckling.

"He sure did," verified Sophie. "I saw him let it out of his crayon box."

"I ain't done nuthin'," contradicted George Sampson, "I ain't done nuthin'."

"I suppose you mean you haven't done anything," suggested the teacher calmly. "If you wish to say something please speak correctly or not at all."

George Sampson did not know what to say to this so he kept still. The teacher continued to speak clearly and emphatically addressing her remarks to the whole group. "It's perfectly all right if he did bring the grasshopper—it's perfectly all right. The grasshopper is our subject for Science that we'll have this afternoon. She picked up the program, looked at it and went on. "Yes we have Science this afternoon. George Sampson is thinking about his science lesson which is very nice."

The children looked at each other and grinned. Sophie and Helen tucked their heads down and laughed and cast sly glances at George Sampson.

"Yes," repeated the teacher, "George Sampson is thinking about his Science." So saying she carefully took the grasshopper from under the box top and held him up by his hind legs. "This is a nice large grasshopper, too," she went on, "a good specimen. See he's chewing tobacco. Now this afternoon we'll learn what we mean by a grasshopper chewing tobacco."

Then she put the grasshopper in the glass tumbler and held her hand over it. The children watched her in wonderment. Then she took a piece of the stem of the sunflower with a leaf on it, slipped it into the tumbler, placed a piece of manila paper over the tumbler, slipped a rubber band around the paper and punched holes in it with her pencil saying, "The grasshopper must have air you know."

The children stretched their eyes and looked and looked. George Sampson was dumbfounded and stupefied. He did not know what to make of it. He did not expect the tables to be turned on him.

Miss Wrice stood back and surveyed the grasshopper with satisfaction and then said, "Now we'll have a nice specimen for our science. I'll punch a few more holes so he'll get plenty of air."

The children looked at George Sampson and kind of chuckled to themselves.

The teacher went on, "Now I'm going to leave a note telling Miss Smith how interested George

Sampson is in his science an' that he had 100 in his science today. Now we'll talk about the grasshopper this afternoon an' maybe we'll draw it. Anyhow I'll draw it on the board for you. Put your things up—it's almost noon time."

Helen and Sophie could scarcely refrain from laughing out loud. Thomas and Robert were sorely disappointed.

George Sampson grinned sheepishly as he got on the line. He shifted from foot to foot.

The little girls looked at each other and tucked their heads down and chuckled.

The boys looked puzzled.

"She sure is a pain, ain't she?" whispered Thomas to George Sampson.

"Yeh," sighed George Sampson, "but anyway I got 100 in Science."

GEORGE SAMPSON AND THE
WILD GEESE

"Good morning, Miss Green, how are you?" greeted Miss Smith as she reached the second floor hall bright and early Monday morning.

"Oh I feel pretty fair," said Miss Green. "What's the news?"

"Oh I don't know much," replied Miss Smith. "I'm gonna get the apprentice this morning. She'll stay two weeks. I hope that George Sampson won't upset things. Last term when the apprentice was in here he tried his best to show off an' kept me under a constant nervous strain. You know how they like to show off when anybody comes in the room an' especially that George Sampson. Then you can't set down on him so well with the apprentice in the room an' he takes any little occasion to start up something."

"Oh he's liable as not to try to start something," replied Miss Green. "I wouldn't be surprised at anything he did."

"I moved him up in the front seat Friday," explained Miss Smith, "so I can keep my eye on him an' he won't have a chance to move. Well I'd better go in an' put some work on the board so they'll have something to do when they come in."

"You certainly believe in putting work on the board," smiled Miss Green.

"Yes," replied Miss Smith, "I always have work on the board when they come in so they'll waste less time an' get into less trouble."

Miss Smith proceeded to put the work on the board, five examples in column addition. The children were to add the examples and check them by subtracting each addend from the sum until the answer was zero. The children liked to do this because of the puzzle element in it and the satisfaction of checking their own results.

As Miss Smith was placing the work on the board, Miss Ross, the apprentice teacher came in, handed her program to Miss Smith and said that she would be in the room two weeks. Miss Ross was a striking looking, slender, brown-skinned young woman with thick reddish brown hair about the same color as her skin. The children all thought Miss Ross very pretty.

"Well I'm certainly glad to have you," said Miss Smith cordially to Miss Ross, "just make yourself at home. Now there's a vacant locker in the cloakroom. You can put your wraps in there an' I'll clear out the bottom desk drawer so you can put your things in it."

"My what a nice big cloakroom," the apprentice teacher remarked after depositing her wraps in the locker," so large an' airy, an' such a nice large window."

"Yes it is a nice cloakroom" agreed Miss

Smith. "I keep the little table an' chairs in there so the children can go in there an' study together sometimes. Now just take a chair," said Miss Smith indicating a chair beside her desk, "an' make yourself at home. I cleared out the bottom drawer so you can put your things in it. . . . Now just feel free to do as you please. Speak to the children just as I would when you see them doing anything they shouldn't do. Now you can just observe today an' tomorrow you can take the B. Class in one or two subjects. There's the program on the wall. You can copy the program in your notebook so you'll know what comes each day."

"My what a pretty picture," said Miss Ross looking at a brightly colored picture in the middle of the front wall. Such beautiful vivid colors. 'Wild Geese Flying South.' It certainly is a pretty picture."

"I got it on sale at an art store," related Miss Smith, "I think it's real pretty. It's plain an' distinct an' you can see it all the way across the room."

The 8:45 bell rang. The lines came in. The children placed their wraps in the cloakroom and took their seats. Miss Smith stood at the door until the lines were all in. Then, as she went into the room, she remarked to Miss Green that she must keep her eye on George Sampson because if she didn't he would certainly start something.

"That's certainly so," replied Miss Green.

The children looked at Miss Ross in silence as

they took their seats. George Sampson took his seat without a word and looked with all eyes at the apprentice.

"Now children," began Miss Smith, "this is Miss Ross, the apprentice teacher. She is to be with us two weeks. Now I want you to show Miss Ross what nice manners you have an' what good work you can do."

The children looked and listened. George Sampson's eyes grew big and interested. The first day the apprentice teacher "observed," that is, she looked on and noted the methods used by the teacher in discipline, instruction and routine matters. She walked around the room, looked at the charts, the pictures on the wall, the children's papers and took notes upon what she observed.

At the end of the day Miss Smith said to Miss Ross, "Now tomorrow you can take the B. Class in Arithmetic an' Reading. In Arithmetic they are taking up subtraction of fractions. Here's the course of study. Now you don't have to do as I do. Just use your own ideas. In Reading right now they are working on silent reading for speed an' comprehension. These are the readers they're using. If you want to get some readers from the Traveling Library an' use them that's perfectly all right. Now you don't have to do the way I do. Use your own ideas as long as you put over the point."

Miss Ross jotted a few points down in her notebook, went home and worked out twenty-five problems in subtraction of fractions. She also worked out a plan for silent reading. She came early the next morning and placed the arithmetic problems on the board. The arithmetic period was from 9:00 to 9:30.

The arithmetic class went off very well. The children gave strict attention to the apprentice teacher, anxious to see what she was going to do. George Sampson looked and listened with intense interest. He had not "started anything" yet. The children went to the board in groups of five. Each child worked an example. Miss Ross made a list of the children who had difficulty in order to give them individual instruction. After the lesson period Miss Ross gave the children some concrete problems involving the processes in subtraction of fractions which they had just had. These problems were to be collected at 10 o'clock.

While the B. Class was reciting the A. Class was preparing a group of problems in the multiplication of fractions involving cancellation.

After the B. Class had finished their recitation Miss Smith had the A. Class pass to the board in groups of five and place the problems on the board. Miss Ross looked on and at the same time walked around to see what the B. Class was doing.

At 10 o'clock the arithmetic papers were collected.

The children cleared their desks. Miss Smith had a sheet of lined manila paper passed to each child. This they headed and laid aside until such time as they would need it.

The teacher developed the idea of direct and indirect quotations. After some discussion she had various children go to the board and write direct quotations with the equivalent indirect quotations under them. She then called attention to the punctuation of each type of quotation. After this she had the children write five such pairs of quotations on their papers.

While the language lesson was in progress a boy came in with a note from the principal to the effect that the kindergarten teacher, Miss Davis, was having a party and when the children went out to recess they were to go out the side door instead of the front door so they would not have to pass by the kindergarten. Miss Smith explained the procedure to the children. The children passed out through the side door as instructed. George Sampson was still minding his "P's and Q's."

The geography lesson followed immediately after recess. The B. Class was studying South America. The children were making notebooks shaped like South America. In these notebooks they pasted pictures of the products of South America. The pictures were usually cut from magazines or newspapers. George Sampson had five pictures of wild animals which he had cut from the Sunday paper. He was turning and twisting and looking to see if anybody was duly impressed with his pictures.

Miss Ross, who was walking around looking at the children's notebooks, picked up one of George Sampson's animals and asked, "What do we use wild animals for?"

"We puts 'em in th' Zoo an' Circus for peeple to look at," explained George Sampson beaming with enthusiasm, pleased to know that somebody took notice of his animals.

"That's fine," answered Miss Ross.

George Sampson beamed with satisfaction.

The A. Class was studying the manners and customs of the people of Mexico. They were preparing to construct a Mexican village on the sand table and different members of the class were constructing articles from bogus paper and coloring them with wax crayon. Some were making the thatched roof houses, some were making the oxen ploughing the fields while others were constructing the men and women in native costume. The children worked busily and interestedly. Miss Ross looked on.

The first bell rang for the noon dismissal. Each child carefully placed his work in a brown envelope which he had made for the purpose. Miss Ross asked Sam Smith, who was going to the store, to bring her a bottle of orange juice and a ham sandwich for her lunch and come back quickly because she had to go out in the yard at 12:30 as this was her day on yard duty.

The children who were going home or to the store lined up and passed out. George Sampson was still "walking straight," Those children who brought their lunches ate them in the room and remained in the room until 12:30. Miss Smith and Miss Ross finished their lunches. Miss Ross went on out into the yard. Miss Smith put the work on the board for the children to take up after they came in from the noon intermission.

The work consisted of a short poem which the children were to copy in their poetry notebooks for future reference.

As Miss Smith was putting the poem on the board, Marcella, a girl from Room One who had been helping the kindergarten teacher with the party came in and brought Miss Smith a dish of ice cream with a piece of waxed paper over it and a little wooden spoon on the top of it. Marcella asked where Miss Ross was. Miss Smith replied that Miss Ross was out in the yard on yard duty. Marcella said she would bring Miss Ross a dish of ice cream just before the bell rang.

Miss Smith sat down and ate her ice cream with the little wooden spoon.

Just before the first bell rang Marcella came back with a large quantity of ice cream in a drinking glass with waxed paper over it and a little wooden spoon on top of the waxed paper and placed it on the desk for Miss Ross.

The second bell rang and the lines came in. The children placed their wraps in the cloakroom, took their seats and looked on the board to see what was to be done.

George Sampson saw the drinking glass of ice cream with the waxed paper on top of it, ducked his head down, laughed, caught several other children's attention and pointed to it. Then he began copying his poem after a fashion. Some of the other children saw the ice cream with the little wooden spoon and looked at each other and laughed as they went about their work. In a few minutes Miss Ross came in and took off her wraps. Thelma immediately stepped up and inquired, "Miss Ross, don't you want me to put your coat an' hat up for you?"

"Yes thank you," replied Miss Ross.

So Thelma took the coat and hat daintily and tipped into the cloakroom. George Sampson ducked his head down and laughed and looked at the other children and pointed to the apprentice teacher on the sly and whispered, "That's for hu."

"That" referred to the ice cream.

Miss Ross went over to the desk to take her notebook from the drawer. Miss Smith whispered to Miss Ross that the ice cream in the glass was for her, that Miss Davis, the kindergarten teacher had sent it up from the kindergarten party.

"My how nice," whispered Miss Ross, "I certainly appreciate it. But how can I eat it with them all looking right in my mouth. Just look how George Sampson is looking."

"That boy's working with one eye on the ice

cream and one eye on his work and is just waiting to start something and upset things," thought Miss Smith.

"Yes, that's right," she answered to Miss Ross. Then she suggested, "Why don't you take it in the cloakroom an' eat it."

"But how can I get it in the cloakroom without them seeing me?" pondered Miss Ross.

Miss Smith thought for a moment, looked around, and noted the picture of wild geese on the wall. Then she and Miss Ross consulted together for a few minutes. George Sampson kept one eye on his work and one eye on the ice cream in the glass, half laughing to himself and straining his ears to hear what was being said.

"I tell you what," whispered Miss Smith to Miss Ross, "their science lesson comes next. Their next topic is the 'Value of Birds.' They're finishing up the lesson they had last week. We'll have a little discussion first an' then when I tell them to look at the picture an' see what kind of birds they are an' what they are doing you take the ice cream an' go on in the cloakroom with it."

George Sampson strained his ears to hear what was being said but could decipher nothing. He kept eyeing the glass of ice cream with the little wooden spoon on top of it.

The children had about finished the work on the board. Miss Smith stood up and asked, "How many have finished copying the poem?"

Most of the children raised their hands. Then she told them to put their poetry notebooks away and take out their bird notebooks. The children did as instructed. Miss Smith then turned around and wrote on the board the subject for discussion. —"The Value of Birds." The children had previously studied about birds and had discussed charts, pictures and specimens from the museum. They had made a class bird book where the best compositions, clippings and pictures were pasted. Each child also had his own bird book. The children vied with each other in trying to have something to go into the class bird book.

Miss Ross stood in readiness to escape with the ice cream.

George Sampson looked at the board.

"Now you may read the subject, Thelma," said Miss Smith.

Thelma read the subject.

George Sampson looked on listlessly. Then his eyes wandered around to see how things in general were going. He felt that something was in the air but he didn't know exactly what.

The children looked at the board in anticipation of what was to be done.

Miss Ross was in readiness to retreat with the ice cream.

"What do we mean by value?" asked Miss Smith.

George Sampson raised his hand and answered, "It means what they good for."

"That's right," said Miss Smith. "Now what is one thing that birds are good for?" continued the teacher. "You remember the chart we had from the museum last week showed us a number of things that birds are good for."

"Food," answered Sam.

"What birds are good for food?" asked Miss Smith.

"Chickens, ducks, pigeons, geese," replied Sophie.

The discussion continued. Other children contributed their part to the recitation. Jesse said birds were good to carry messages and good for pets. Thomas said they were good to destroy bugs and worms that eat up the vegetables, Robert said they eat up dead things and help keep the city clean.

"We call those scavengers," put in Miss Smith.

George Sampson's mind wandered from the discussion in hand back to the glass of ice cream and he laughed to himself as he saw Miss Ross standing with her hand on the glass of ice cream.

After the discussion had progressed far enough Miss Smith pointed to the picture overhead and said, "Now look at the picture an' see what kind of birds they are an' what they are good for."

The children centered all eyes on the picture, George Sampson looked up eagerly forgetting all about the ice cream.

At that moment Miss Ross seized the dish of

ice cream and the little wooden spoon and disappeared into the cloakroom.

George Sampson was still concentrating on the picture.

Shortly George Sampson raised his hand to tell what kind of birds they were and exclaimed enthusiastically, "Them is wild geese flyin' South an they good f'food an' they feathers are pretty."

"Yes that's right," replied the teacher. "Now in your notebooks I want you to write a composition telling about 'The Value of Birds.' Make your outline first and have a paragraph for each point in your outline."

The children set to work. George Sampson took a little breathing space and looked around to see what was going on. He looked around the room to see where the apprentice teacher was but no apprentice teacher was in sight. Then he remembered the little dish of ice cream with the little wooden spoon on top of it and looked all around but saw no trace of it. He looked from side to side and from the back to the front of the room for the apprentice teacher and the glass of ice cream but they were nowhere to be seen.

GEORGE SAMPSON GETS PUT UP

The first Tuesday in September, the opening day of school, rolled around again. George Sampson and Lottie were highly excited as they got ready for school. Each had a brand new outfit in which to start back to school. Lottie's outfit consisted of a pink dress, brown slippers and pink socks. George Sampson had a new brown suit and a blue waist and black shoes.

Mrs. Brite and Granny admonished Lottie and George Sampson to make a good start in their lessons and to have good conduct.

"I wonda if she's gonna put me up?" fretted George Sampson. "She betta put me up 'cause she didn't put me up last time."

"Now don start worryin'," advised Granny, "but jis wait an' see how things come out an' act nice an' pay attention to th' teecha."

So George Sampson and Lottie started out, lunches under arm and pencil boxes in hand. As they neared the school they were joined by Thelma, Thomas Brown, Rosie and her little sister, Millie, all bubbling over with enthusiasm after their long vacation.

"I wonder if we'll get put up?" they speculated to George Sampson and Lottie.

"I think I'll get put up," said Lottie confidentially.

"She betta put me up," ejaculated George Sampson, " 'cause she didn't put me up last time." The "she" referred to Miss Smith.

They reached the school yard. The children were gathered around in little groups greeting each other and telling their vacation experiences. Shortly the bell rang and the children went to the same rooms in which they had been at the close of school, took seats and anxiously waited to see if they were going to "get put up."

The teachers greeted each other and shook hands with the principal.

Miss Herman was not back as she had taken a leave of absence for the year to study Music. Miss Reese, a very efficient substitute teacher, was in her place. The children looked and looked, on seeing a new person but Miss Reese soon had them quiet and busy. She explained to them that Miss Herman was going to be away this year studying Music and that she was to be their teacher. This settled the children's minds.

About 10 o'clock the principal started around with the promotion lists and began moving the children from room to room. All of the children in Room One had graduated the previous June. This necessitated all of the children in each room, except the few who were so very far behind the others, being moved up.

About 10:30 the principal reached Miss Smith's

room and read the list of pupil's who were to be promoted to the next room, formerly Miss Herman's room, now Miss Reese's room.

George Sampson sat tense on the edge of his seat as the names of his classmates were called one after another. He strained his ears to hear his name but it was not called. Each child got in line as his name was called. In a few minutes all of the children were on line except George Sampson and four others, two of whom had been absent because of illness.

"Now these children, come with me," said the principal to the children who were lined up.

The children marched out and left George Sampson and his four companions among the empty seats. George Sampson rolled his eyes at the teacher and turned his back and muttered to himself that he was gonna tell his mother all right enough, as the tears rolled down his cheeks. The other four children were downcast but resigned. Those who had been absent had not expected to be promoted.

Shortly the principal returned bringing the children from the room below and had them line up around the room. Miss Smith told the children to fill up the vacant seats. When all the seats were filled five children were still standing. There were no seats left for them. Miss Smith had them each take a seat with another child.

By noon the general moving up had been completed. Immediately after the lunch period the principal sent around a sheet of paper on which each teacher was to write the number of pupils in the room and the number of seats. Miss Reese had 43 children and 48 seats while Miss Smith had 53 children and 48 seats.

Shortly the principal came into Miss Smith's room and called the 5 children who had not been promoted and told them with special emphasis to George Sampson that they were to be put in Miss Reese's room on 5 week's trial because Miss Smith's room was so crowded; but if they did not do their work and have good conduct Miss Reese would put them back at the end of the 5 weeks.

George Sampson's face lighted up with joy and in his heart he resolved for the moment that he would "turn over a new leaf." He was overjoyed at the idea of being "put up" on any terms. The other four children were much pleased and said "Yes sir," with alacrity. So the five were duly ushered into Miss Reese's room and given seats. That evening Miss Smith told Miss Reese about the children who had been promoted on trial dwelling on the history of George Sampson.

When school was dismissed George Sampson, in high spirits, met Lottie at the gate and greeted her with, "I got put up, did you?"

Lottie replied that she did.

Then he rushed home ahead of Lottie, burst into the kitchen door telling Granny that he had been promoted to Miss Reese's room, a new teacher who was nice, not a thing like Miss Smith.

He neglected to say however, that he was promoted only on five weeks trial and that if he did not keep up with his class and have good conduct he would have to go back into Miss Smith's room at the end of the first five weeks.

The first day the teachers had simply enrolled the children and gotten the records straight. The second day they began to organize the classes, arrange routine matters and assign the children work to do.

Miss Reese had ten words placed on the blackboard. These she had the children divide into syllables, pronounce and explain. She called attention to the difficult part of each word.

Each child was passed a notebook in which to copy the words. Miss Reese instructed the children to take their notebooks home and learn how to spell the words.

Miss Reese then gave the children permanent seats and appointed monitors. George Sampson was appointed monitor of the ball and bat and his joy was complete. Miss Reese, having been informed of George Sampson's history by Miss Smith, thought that making him a monitor would serve as "an ounce of prevention."

George Sampson went home the second day in higher spirits than ever and told his mother and grandmother that he was monitor of the ball and bat and that he liked Miss Reese better than Miss Smith because she wasn't always fussin' at him and looking at him so hard.

"She's real sweet," put in Lottie.

Miss Reese had a quiet soothing disposition, yet was firm and positive. Her temperament did not clash with George Sampson's. She had various little devices to keep things running smoothly. One device was a conduct chart which hung on the wall. This chart was made of a large piece of one fourth inch squared paper pasted on cardboard. On the extreme left hand side of the chart the children's names were written alphabetically in a column, each name on a line. The remainder of the chart was blank. Whenever a child created any form of disorder a check was placed opposite his name. Sometimes if the disorder were excessive two or more checks were placed by the name. The fewer checks a child had by his name the better his conduct was. The children took great interest in studying the chart before school and at recess and noon and comparing their records with those of their neighbors. Whenever the checks beside any child's name extended all the way across the chart the teacher would place a new sheet on top of the old one, pasting it only at the top edge so that it could be lifted up and the one below could be seen.

George Sampson got along fairly well for the first two weeks. He studied his spelling with the aid of Granny and Lottie and his marks ranged between 75 and 80 which was very good for him. He did fairly well in his other subjects. He got only three checks by his name on the conduct chart. This was not excessive in comparison with some of the other children's records. But, sad to say, the next two weeks he began to slip up a little and to slide back to his old tricks, teasing the children and punching and poking at them. Right doing was becoming dull and monotonous to him. His spelling marks descended to 40 and 50. His other lessons fell off. He was reported twice by teachers on yard duty for infractions of the rules, once for getting water after the bell had rung and once for chasing a boy all over the yard instead of getting on the line promptly.

The second time he was reported Miss Reese kept him after school and told him that he was slipping back in his work and conduct and she wanted him to improve and study his spelling at home and give attention to his other lessons and watch his conduct in the yard because, as he knew, he was only promoted on trial, and if he did not keep up he would have to go back into Miss Smith's room at the end of the first five weeks.

George Sampson looked sorry and said, "Yessum."

The next morning George Sampson rose early and he and Lottie reached school before 8:30. He had made up his mind to do better because he certainly did not want to go back into Miss Smith's room. He did not go on the playground for fear he might not hear the bell and get into his room on time; but went on into the boys' yard and began chasing first one boy and then another.

Suddenly he faced around and discovered a new boy on the scene, a stout country looking boy in overalls. The new boy was running after another boy. In the course of his running he ran out into the street.

Miss Jones, a first floor teacher who was on yard duty, called the new boy and told him to play in the yard and not run out into the street.

"Wellum," replied the boy pleasantly.

"What did you say?" asked the teacher.

"Wellum," repeated the boy.

"He means, 'Yessum,' " explained the boy who was playing with him.

George Sampson, who was standing listening, laughed out loud. After the teacher had gone to another part of the yard George Sampson ran up behind the new boy, hooted, "Wellum, wellum, wellum," in a mimicking voice, snatched the boy's hat, hit him on the head and ran with the hat.

The new boy was infuriated. He chased George Sampson, got his hat back and hit George Sampson a telling blow. A fight ensued. Miss Jones stopped the fight, took George Sampson up to his room and reported him to his teacher. Miss Reese looked at him reproachfully and told him to stay in at recess.

After all the children had passed out at recess Miss Reese called George Sampson up to the desk and asked, "Now George Sampson what do you mean by teasing a boy an' starting a fight out in the yard? You know you were reported twice last week an' you've been doing very poorly in your work here lately. I'm afraid you'll have to go back if you don't do a lot of improving in the next week. You know you were promoted on five week's trial and you only have one week left. Today is the fourth Friday and next Friday ends the five weeks. Now the other children who came up with you are keeping up with the class nicely but you're slipping further and further back."

Poor George Sampson looked penitent, hung his head and resolved to himself that he would try to do better. After recess he worked diligently at his geography and language. After noon he worked with equal diligence at his other lessons. He copied his spelling words down carefully on a piece of paper as he had misplaced his notebook, and put them in his back pocket resolving to take them home and study them.

As it looked very much like rain the bell for dismissal rang a little earlier and Miss Reese cautioned the children to hurry home. George Sampson felt in his back pocket to be sure his spelling words were there.

On his way home, however, he snatched a boy's hat and ran. The boy ran after him and in the scramble the spelling words fell from George Sampson's pocket and were lost.

Friday evening a severe storm occurred. The wind blew violently, accompanied by thunder and lightning and hail. Windows were broken in many houses; a number of trees were blown down, among them a large tree on the playground.

Monday morning was bright and crisp and sunshiny. George Sampson was full of high spirits and activity. He and Lottie raced to school. George Sampson reached school first, leaped over to the playground and began snatching boys' hats and running. Then he spied the tree that had been blown down and the children crowded around it. He rushed over to the tree, got into the middle of the scene, and began jumping up and down on the trunk of the tree. Presently the first bell rang and the children ran from the playground into the yard to get on the line. George Sampson and two other boys, however, remained on the playground with the tree.

As the children were doing their "morning work" Miss Reese looked out of the window and spied George Sampson standing on the tree and sent a large boy out to tell him to come in immediately. George Sampson grabbed the boy's hat and ran all around before coming in, thereby getting five more checks by his name.

As he entered the room he remembered that he was on trial until Friday and he went sheepishly to his seat and started his "morning work."

Shortly after the tardy bell rang a new boy with a closely shaven head entered bringing a transfer card.

"Good morning," greeted the teacher kindly looking at the card, "your name is Henry Snipe?"

"Yes'm" replied the boy.

George Sampson noted the closely shaven head, ducked down and laughed to himself. At recess he waited until the line was safely out of doors then he smacked Henry Snipe on the head and danced all around yelling, "Snip—snipe—snew!"

George Sampson's followers and admirers, Thomas, Robert and Jesse did the same. Henry Snipe was highly incensed. He drew his fist back and knocked George Sampson down. George Sampson jumped up, grabbed the boy around the neck and threw him to the ground. The dust flew in four different directions. The teacher on yard duty rushed up and took hold of them and escorted them both to Miss Reese and reported them.

Henry Snipe told how he was out in the yard playing when George Sampson grabbed his hat, smacked him on the head, called him, "Snip—snipe—snew" and ran with his hat.

Miss Reese knew that this ran true to form.

She looked at George Sampson reproachfully and asked, "What is the matter with you, George Sampson? What did I tell you Friday? Now this morning you were behind the lines an' Friday you were fighting an' now you are reported for fighting again."

"I was jis 'nitiatin' him," explained George Sampson regretfully.

"You know you have no business hitting anyone on the head," said the teacher. "Now you will have five more checks by your name an' I'm very much afraid you'll have to go back into Miss Smith's room Friday."

Thelma and Sophie looked at each other and laughed and whispered, "His space'll soon be filled out all the way across."

George Sampson went to his seat in low spirits with apparitions of Miss Smith's piercing eyes staring at him and her finger pointing in his face. He tried to concentrate his mind on his lessons with little success.

Time wore on. Finally the bell rang for the noon intermission. George Sampson took his place on the line slowly and dejectedly. He went home in low spirits, ate very little lunch and had very little to say.

"What is th' matta wid you, George Sampson?" demanded Granny. "Why ain't you eatin' no lunch an' why ain't you sayin' nuthin'?"

"I don feel so good," groaned George Sampson more or less truthfully.

"Maybe y'oughta stay home," suggested Granny.

"No'am I don wanna stay home," sighed George Sampson, "I don wanna miss my lessons."

Granny looked in surprise at this unusual procedure but said, "All right whin you git home this evening I'll give you some medicine if you ain't betta."

George Sampson got through the afternoon somehow. When he reached home he told his grandmother that he was feeling better. He had no desire to take any medicine.

Meanwhile some of the children had told Lottie that George Sampson was gonna get put back because he was always missing his lessons and always making trouble and starting fights and coming in late and Miss Reese said she was gonna put him back Friday because the five weeks would be up Friday and he had only been put up on five weeks trial.

When George Sampson went to the store Lottie told Granny what the children had said and added that she thought that was why George Sampson was acting like he was sick.

"Well don say nuthin' t'him 'bout it," cautioned Granny. "Wait 'til yo Ma comes. She oughta be home pretty soon."

"Yes'm," replied Lottie.

Mrs. Brite came home shortly. George Sampson had not yet returned from the store. Lottie peered out of the door to make sure he was not in sight. Then she and Granny told Mrs. Brite of the prospect of George Sampson being "put back."

"Oh my goodness!" exclaimed Mrs. Brite, "I hope she don put him back 'cause he was put back once already last year. He ain't gittin' nowhere doin' nuthin' but gittin' put back."

"That's right," agreed Granny.

George Sampson returned from the store with the groceries. He was not in his usual high spirits.

"How is you, George Sampson?" asked his mother. "Granny tells me y'ain't feelin' so good."

George Sampson fearing that he would have to take some medicine attempted to brighten up a little and said that he was feeling better.

"An what's this I hear 'bout you gonna git put back?" questioned his mother. "Me workin' myself to death to send you to school an' give you a eddication an' you ain't doin' nuthin' but gittin' put back."

George Sampson began whimpering and crying and mumbled, "The teecha say she's gonna put me back in Miss Smith's room 'cause a new boy come an' started up a fight wid me an' the teecha said she's gonna put me back in Miss Smith's 'cause I was jis put up on trial. But that ole boy started up th' fight an' th' teecha thought it was me."

"You didn't tell me you was jis put up on trial," rebuked his mother. "I hope to heaven she don put you back in that Miz Smith's room. I thought you said you was doin' all right—I thought you was th' monitor a th' ball an' bat."

"Yessum I is monitor a th' ball an' bat," affirmed George Sampson, "but them chil'rin's alays startin' up things wid me an' th' teecha thinks it's me an' takes offa my deportment mark—an' I don wanna go back in Miz Smith's room 'cause she don lak me." And with this he began to cry afresh and mumbled, "Maybe if you go ova an' see hu maybe she won't put me back."

The "hu" referred to Miss Reese.

"Now look here, George Sampson," frowned his mother, "you stop all that fightin' an' carryin' on an' git them lessons. I ain't sendin' you to no school t'git put back all th' time. An' b'sides I can't git ova there till Thursdee. An' b'sides what good is it f'me to go ova there if you don study yo lesson. Now I'm comin' ova there Thursdee an' after that I *ain't comin' ova there no mo.*"

George Sampson went back to school the next day and tried to do better with varying degrees of success.

In spite of good resolutions he tickled a new girl, Rosalee, on the neck with a feather. The little girl immediately raised her hand and reported him to the teacher. Miss Reese promptly put three more checks by George Sampson's name. He protested it was just an accident but the checks remained, much to George Sampson's consternation.

He thought of what his mother had said and tried to settle down to work. Things went well for awhile. Then a boy's paper blew across the room and landed directly under George Sampson's seat. He could not resist the temptation. His foot went down on the paper just as the boy was preparing to pick it up. The boy promptly reported him to the teacher who placed three more checks beside his name.

"How'd y'git 'long today, George Sampson?" asked Granny that evening as he and Lottie were fooling around the kitchen.

"I gits along all right," grumbled George Sampson, "but them otha chil'rin keep bothering me an' th' teecha thinks it's me an' keeps puttin' checks by my name an' talkin' lak she's gonna put me back. I'll be glad when Mama goes ova there t'see hu."

"Well yo Ma's goin' ova there Thursdee whin she gits off—but George Sampson you gotta stop so much foolishness an' study yo lesson 'cause it ain't no good a yo Ma goin' ova there if you ain't gonna study yo lesson."

"Yessum," answered George Sampson humbly.

So George Sampson made an honest effort to do better. All day Wednesday he gave strict attention to his lessons and conduct. Thursday morning he made 100 in Arithmetic and got no checks by his name which was a good thing because only two more spaces opposite his name remained blank. After noon he got right on to his geography and diligently drew his map.

About 2 o'clock Mrs. Brite reached the school, met the principal in the hall, and was directed to Miss Reese's room.

Miss Reese saw someone out in the hall looking in the door. She told the children to go on with their work and stepped out into the hall to investigate.

"I'm George Sampson's mutha," explained Mrs. Brite to the teacher.

"How do you do Mrs. Brite," greeted Miss Reese extending her hand.

"Fine, I thank you. How is yo'self?" replied Mrs. Brite. "I jis come ova t'see how George Sampson is gittin' 'long wid his lessons. He tells me sompin' 'bout he's gonna git put back."

"Well he's not doing so well," began Miss Reese, "you know he was just put up on five weeks trial because Miss Smith's room was so crowded, he an' four others. Now the others are doing very nicely but George Sampson isn't doing as he should and his time's up tomorrow an' I'm afraid he won't be able to stay in here."

"Well what is th' trouble wid him," puzzled Mrs. Brite, "ain't he got no brains?"

"Oh yes, his brain is all right an' he can do when he wants to," replied Miss Reese, "but he just wastes his time with foolishness an' he likes to pick fights with the other children an' teases them an' of course you know he can't keep his mind on his work an' carry on a lot of foolishness. Now I have a chart where I keep a record of their conduct." Here she called and had a little girl bring the chart from the wall and then explained, "Now you see here is the chart. Each check means some misconduct. You see he has more checks than any of the other children. His conduct has been so poor an' he's been wasting so much time I don't see how he can keep up with the class."

"Well I sho hopes he can stay in yo room," sighed Mrs. Brite, " 'cause he thinks so much of you. Yes'm he's jis crazy 'bout you. He talks 'bout you all th' time. He say 'Mamma she ain't lak that otha teecha. She don fuss at me an' look at me so hard an' she lets me take charge a th' ball an' bat an' I laks hu betta than any teecha I ever had an' I jis hopes I gits t'stay in there.' —Yes'm he jis lubs you."

"Well now of course George Sampson isn't so bad," mused Miss Reese, "that is he isn't mean or malicious or anything like that—just mischievous. He's good hearted an' all an' if he'd put his mind on his work he'd be able to keep up very nicely. But of course with a room full of children I can't just keep right after him all the time. But I'll see what can be done. Maybe if I keep him another five weeks he might get settled."

"Yes'm—well I certainly hopes you keeps him 'cause he's so fond of you. Yes'm he jis lubs you an' that's th' main reason I hopes he gits t'stay in yo room an' I'll make him study his home work every day."

"Well Mrs. Brite I'll see what can be done."

"All right Miss Reese. Good-bye."

"Good-bye, Mrs. Brite."

And George Sampson was not put back.

CASE 999 — A CHRISTMAS STORY

CASE 999—
A CHRISTMAS STORY

By

ANNE SCOTT
Author of *George Sampson Brite*

BOSTON
MEADOR PUBLISHING COMPANY
PUBLISHERS

PRINTED IN THE UNITED STATES OF AMERICA

THE MEADOR PRESS, BOSTON, MASSACHUSETTS

Note: The names of all persons are fictitious. The places are fictitious. The characters are fictitious. The plot is fictitious. The incidents are fictitious.

CASE 999 — A CHRISTMAS STORY

CASE 999 — A CHRISTMAS STORY

Christmas was descending rapidly. It was descending on mansion and hovel alike. It was descending everywhere. Shoppers were scurrying frantically around with red packages sticking out of shopping bags. Storekeepers were setting Christmas trees outside their shops and stacking their windows with candies and nuts. The churches were busy rehearsing Christmas carols. Children were racing back and forth practicing for Christmas programs. Yes, Christmas was descending everywhere.

It was descending on the broken down, unsanitary, exorbitant renting tenement that housed eighteen Negro families in a side section of the great city. It was descending down into the damp, dark, musty cellar "apartment" of this tenement where Granny and Sammie lived or rather existed. It was descending on the little brown church around the corner, where Reverend Jones, the devoted Negro pastor, administered to the spiritual needs of his little flock.

9

It was descending on the drug store across
the street over which young Doctor Ross
lived and kept his office. It descended on
Miss Rose, the social worker, who in spite
of her education and culture still remembered hard times. — Christmas was descending everywhere.

It descended on the little juvenile gang
that Sammie went out snatching pocket
books with. It descended on the other Negro families in the rat infested tenement
with its disgraceful plumbing, or lack of
plumbing, its dug-out court yard and its unsanitary out-door toilets. Yes, Christmas
was descending everywhere.

"Come in, Brotha Jones," exclaimed
Granny frantically, dish rag in hand, as she
jerked open the gunny-sack-bound door of
her two-room dark, dank cellar "apartment."
"What did dem judges at de court say bout
my Sammie? —Tell me quick —Tell me—
Is dey gonna take my boy way from me? —
Is dey? — I won't let 'em — He's all I got
lef an' I ain't gonna let 'em take him."

"All right, all right — now sit down, sit
down, an' I'll tell you everything," soothed
Reverend Jones.

Granny, breathing hard, sat down on a broken backed chair while the pastor sat on a large wooden box and put his feet on a smaller box to keep the rats from running over them.

Then he went on, "I talked with the juvenile authorities and they said Sammie was with some boys that were snatching pocket books an' they took those that they caught down to the Detention House. — The boys seemed afraid to talk. — I don't think they caught them all. — Deacon Woods an' Deacon Smith went down with me an' we talked with the authorities a long time."

"My Sammie's a good boy," sobbed Granny. "I know he wooden do nuthin lak that ef them otha boys hadnta made him do it.—I jus know he wooden."

"Now, now," calmed the preacher. "Of course Sammie's a good boy but he gets in with bad company—course his mother an father are both dead an it's kinda hard for you to keep up with him with your rheumatism an asthma an all.—Now maybe if he were put in a foster home way away from those boys—maybe he would get along better an it would be easier for you."

Here Granny jumped up, stamped her

foot, threw down the dish rag and cried out, "I ain't gonna let him go.—It ain't his fault his fatha an mothas dead.—Dey killed his motha in de riot an put his fatha in de pen'-tentry for takin up for his self an den killed him afta dey got him in there."

"Now you don't know that, Granny," interrupted the preacher.

"Well, somebodee hit him on d'head an broke his skull an who done it?"

"The Lord only knows," sighed Reverend Jones, "the Lord only knows.—Now don't get yourself all worked up, Granny— they're gonna let me take charge of Sammie —they're gonna turn Sammie over to me an I'm gonna do all I can to keep him straight but if he gets in trouble again I'm afraid they'll take him an put him in a foster home an I won't be able to stop them.—I had to talk up a mighty lot to get them to parole Sammie to me.—An I'm gonna do the best I can for him—you can be sure of that."

Here Granny put the dish rag up to her face and wept and her whole body shook with emotion as she sobbed out, "Brotha Jones, you is a good man—you is a Christian man an I'm gonna pray for you ebry day a' my life but I ain't gonna let my Sammie go.

—He's all I got lef in dis world.—I'll die befo I'll let em take him.—Brotha Jones pray dat nuthin happens to my Sammie.—Pray dat dey neva take him away from me."

"Now, now, Granny, calm yourself, calm yourself—I'm praying for Sammie all the time."

A loud silence followed. Then the preacher commented: "It's getting a little colder—maybe we'll have snow for Christmas."

At this juncture Miss Rose, the social worker came in with her little black zipper notebook under her arm with a record of Granny's and Sammie's case therein—Case 999. Granny tried to spruce up when the social worker came in.

Miss Rose sensed that something was wrong. She and the minister shook hands and exchanged glances.

"Set down," said Granny embarrassedly, "I used to hab some nice chairs befo my trouble but I ain't got none now."

Granny always referred to the riot as her trouble. She spoke of things in terms of before and after her trouble.

"That's all right," replied Miss Rose. "I'll just sit on this stool—I'm tryin' to find you

a better place but you know how hard places
are to get."

"Yes'm, dats right," agreed Granny. The
preacher looked meditatively off into space.

"Well, how are you getting along?" asked
Miss Rose after a pause.

"I need some coal for my stove," explained
Granny, "coal go so fast dis weatha.—Doc
Ross sent me some medicine fo my ashma.—
It's he'ped me already."

"Well—all right," said Miss Rose as she
wrote out the order for the coal. "Be careful with that stove an let in a little fresh air
every once in a while to ventilate."

"Yes'm, I will," answered Granny. "I hab
to keep dem rags stuffed in de windas to keep
de wind out cause dey won't fix de winda
panes."

"Well, I'll see what I can do about that,"
said Miss Rose.—I'll stop in an see Dr. Ross
when I leave here. His office is up over the
drug store isn't it?"

"Yes'm, he libs right cross there up ova
de drug store.—He's a nice young man—jus
as mannerable as he kin be."

"Well, that's fine," returned Miss Rose.
Here's two tickets to the Christmas Festival
for you an Sammie. The carfare tickets are

on there.—How is Sammie getting along?"

Granny broke out crying and shook with sobs. Reverend Jones turned toward the social worker and began to explain in an even tone of voice that Sammie had been in a little trouble but everything's gonna be all right.

"There's nothing for Granny to worry about," explained the pastor. "I'm gonna look out for Sammie an everything's gonna be all right."

Miss Rose sensed the situation and agreed, "Yes, Sammie's a fine boy an I know Reverend Jones'll take good care of him.—Now I'm going on but I'll be back in a couple of days. Don't worry—Sammie'll be all right."

Granny said nothing but looked tearfully at the dirt floor of her cellar "apartment."

"I'm going too, Granny." said the minister, "but I'll be back soon."

As they tramped across the court yard in the snow Miss Rose remarked that she had heard what an eloquent speaker Reverend Jones was.

"I try to give my people a few thoughts," replied Reverend Jones modestly. "I take a course every now and then and try to keep up with the times."

Then he began and told the social worker some things about Sammie's case.

"Well, now don't you think," asked the social worker earnestly, "that it really would be better for Granny to go to the Infirmary and Sammie to a foster home?—She's too old to really keep up with Sammie and she's half sick all the time from being down in that cellar.—That's what makes Sammie so bad. —That place gives me the creeps.—I've been trying to get them another place but you know how hard that is—and our budget is so limited.—I had a hard time to get them those two second-hand beds. They had been sleeping on the floor.—They pay $15 a month for that place.—It should be against the law for anybody to live there. Why the water just drips. Sometimes it doesn't run at all. Sometimes the whole building freezes up and they have to go blocks to get water.—Those rotten sinks are overrun with roaches. The coal oil lamps are dangerous too. The agent won't turn on the electricity.—Sammie doesn't get enough air and sunlight and in his subconscious mind he resents his surroundings.—There's no way to find them another place in these times—the housing shortage being what it is. The only thing to do as I can see is to put him in a foster home and send her to the Infirmary.—Sammie has nothing to take up his leisure time—the other boys don't either for that matter. That's why they went out snatching pocket books. —That man ought not to be allowed to rent those places."

"It's truly a sin," replied the pastor. "It's truly a sin—no way to heat and light properly and no ventilation—and the plumbing's a disgrace—but it would kill Granny to part with Sammie—I really believe it would be the death of her. You see, as I said, she's had Sammie since he was three months old. His mother was killed in the riot and they claimed his father shot a man. But the folks said he was just trying to protect his wife and baby. The father was sent to the penitentiary and died there from a blow on the head. They said it was an accident but the Lord only knows.—On the night of the riot they set the house on fire. Granny managed to wrap Sammie up in a blanket and carried him through a trap door down into the cellar and climbed up on some rubbish piled high in the cellar and on out the back cellar window. She was half choked and blind with smoke and was picked up and taken to the hospital,

. . . "and carried him through a trap door" . . .

she and Sammie—Sammie's mother was shot as she ran out of the house. She was dead and buried before Granny and Sammie got out of the hospital.—The father was sentenced to fifty years in the penitentiary. He didn't have much of a trial. You know how those things go. After about eight years he died from a blow on the head. They said it was an accident. Granny went to visit him at intervals but she never took Sammie or told Sammie much about it.—Sammie's father was her only child. Sammie's all she's got now and she clings to him with a death grip."

Yes, Granny had lived in back rooms, third stories and basement rooms in the twelve years she and Sammie had knocked around together. She had scrubbed office floors at night—taken in washing, worked at odd jobs for a little more than three dollars a week and had done a little of everything to keep body and soul together.

Sammie had sold papers from the time he was six years old and had brought his pennies home to help out. After a while Granny's rheumatism and asthma had become so bad from washing and standing on damp floors that she could not sustain herself and Sammie and so had to apply to the Relief Agency for help.

The Relief Agency investigated and Granny received aid for herself and Sammie.

It was two weeks before Christmas. The eighteen families in the tenement house with Granny and Sammie were scurrying around making ready. Granny pinned two little ten-cent store wreaths up in the cellar windows in spite of the rags stuck in the holes. Sammie swept the dirt floor energetically, replaced the gunny sack at the bottom of the door, cleaned the two lamp chimneys and set the rat trap.

Sammie loved his grandmother and longed for the time when he could take her to a better environment. He was enthusiastic about the Christmas work the children were doing at school. His conduct had improved. He was home early every evening. Twice weekly he went to the minister to get his report card signed. He also had to take a report card in from his class-room teacher to the probation officer.

The teacher was most sympathetic and did all she could to help him without making him feel self-conscious.

But the little gang that Sammie had been with was determined that he would not get away from them. They kept after him. They threatened to beat him up if he tried to get out of the gang. The fact of the matter was they had beaten two or three boys unmercifully and one boy's face had been slashed. The juvenile gangs had become so rampageous that the people were demanding that something be done about it. The police were on the alert at all times for juvenile offenders.

Sammie stood in constant fear of the gang. He tried to evade them as much as he could. He was really afraid to tell anything about them.

In spite of all precautions the gang rounded Sammie up and intimidated him into going on another pocketbook snatching expedition by telling him that they would beat his head in if he didn't go. He went.

Sammie and some of the others were caught and taken into the juvenile court. All of them had been in the court before. Some had been in two or three times. Sammie's

case and the other cases were gone into carefully. The juvenile authorities called the
social worker and the pastor in for a conference.

Reverend Jones and Miss Rose were much
grieved because they had worked so hard
with Sammie and thought that progress had
been made. The school report said that Sammie was a nice boy but he was victim of a
bad environment and bad company.

Sammie wept and begged them not to tell
Granny and said the boys had made him do
it, had threatened to beat his head in if he
didn't.

He said they had already beat up one boy
and slashed his face. The authorities talked
with Sammie, and Sammie promised to do
better.

He was given a report card and told to go
back to school. Then the social worker, the
pastor and the juvenile authorities went into
further conference. The authorities recommended that Sammie be put in a foster home
where he would get the proper supervision
and that Granny be sent to the Infirmary
where she could be cared for. The pastor
finally agreed that this was the best thing to
do and that he would have to be the one to

tell them, but he asked that he be allowed to wait until after Christmas. He said that they were all pepped up to go to the Christmas Festival and that he couldn't find it in his heart to spoil their Christmas—but anyway you took it—it would be the hardest thing he had ever had to do in his whole experience.

No one mentioned anything to Granny about Sammie's latest digression. Sammie tried to act as though nothing had happened but Granny sensed that something was wrong and prayed and prayed and prayed.

Christmas eve. Christmas carols. Candles in windows. Dust-like snow flakes in the air. Stockings in chimneys. Last minute shopping in neighborhood stores.

The eighteen families in the tenement were making preparations for Christmas morning. They all had tickets to the Annual Christmas Festival. The Festival started at 9:30 a.m. and lasted until 9:30 p.m. The ticket entitled the holder to a good dinner; candy, clothing and toys for the children and clothing for the older people. An interesting program of songs, dances and dramatic skits from the different community centers was given. The neighbors were all excited about going and a number of them planned to go together. The pastor planned to go along with the group which included Granny and Sammie.

Granny and Sammie were highly excited. They fixed their "best" clothes and laid them out on the stool. The night was very cold. The temperature was 10 above zero. Granny and Sammie stuffed the rags more tightly into the broken windows and cracks. Sammie put a lump of coal in the stove, then put a sprinkle of ashes on the fire and left the stove door slightly open. Granny put the tickets for the Festival in the holder with the insurance policies. She gave Sammie the presents that she had had the minister purchase for her, a cap and gloves and a stocking with candy and nuts and an orange in it. Sammie's present to Granny was a head scarf to wear to the Festival the next day. Granny looked around to see that everything was in order. Sammie pushed the rat trap into place. Then they went to sleep in anticipation of Christmas morning.

Christmas morning came. The temperature had risen to about 28 degrees and there was a light snow on the ground. A little after nine o'clock some of the neighbors and the pastor and deacons gathered in the court yard of the tenement all ready for the Festival. They yoo-ood for Granny and Sammie but got no response.

"It's a wonder they're not up yet," pondered the minister. "Granny said positively that she and Sammie were going."

"Well, I'll knock on the door," said one of the deacons.

He knocked and knocked but no response. One of the neighbors said he would go around the side and knock on the window. He looked in, knocked and then called out to the others, "They're both asleep and I can't wake 'em up."

Some of the others came around and looked in. The minister pulled out the rags, peered in the window, clapped his hands and tried to rouse them but could not. The neighbors and deacons crowded behind him and tried to see in.

"They is sure sleepin sound," observed someone.

"Well," said the minister after a moment's silence, "I'll call the police and have them open the door."

The police came, forced the door and tried to rouse Granny and Sammie but without success. The policemen looked at each other. Somebody ran across the street for Dr. Ross. The doctor came, shook his head and said they had been dead about eight hours—asphyxiated. Silence fell on the group. They turned away slowly and talked in hushed voices. The pastor shook his head sadly and said to the deacons, "The Lord knows best."

The neighbors gathered around the pastor in awe stricken silence.

"Yes, the Lord knows best," repeated Reverend Jones. "Sammie's been in a lot of trouble with the law lately and the authorities had decided to put Sammie in a foster home and send Granny to the Infirmary after Christmas."

The neighbors all gasped. They well knew Granny and Sammie's story and it would have wrung their hearts to see Granny and Sammie separated.

"Yes," went on the minister, "they'll never know now how near they came to being separated and it's just as well. They had been together since that terrible night of the riot when she carried him through smoke and flames to safety and who knows but that she has carried him through smoke and fumes to safety at last."

ABOUT THE EDITORS

Henry Louis Gates, Jr., is the W. E. B. Du Bois Professor of the Humanities, Chair of the Afro-American Studies Department, and Director of the W. E. B. Du Bois Institute for Afro-American Research at Harvard University. One of the leading scholars of African-American literature and culture, he is the author of *Figures in Black: Words, Signs, and the Racial Self* (1987), *The Signifying Monkey: A Theory of Afro-American Literary Criticism* (1988), *Loose Canons: Notes on the Culture Wars* (1992), and the memoir *Colored People* (1994).

Jennifer Burton is in the Ph.D. program in English Language and Literature at Harvard University. She is the volume editor of *The Prize Plays and Other One-Acts* in this series. She is a contributor to *The Oxford Companion to African-American Literature* and to *Great Lives From History: American Women*. With her mother and sister she coauthored two one-act plays, *Rita's Haircut* and *Litany of the Clothes*. Her creative nonfiction has appeared in *There and Back* and *Buffalo*, the Sunday magazine of the *Buffalo News*.

Marilyn Sanders Mobley is an Associate Professor of English and Director of African American Studies at George Mason University. She is the author of *Folk Roots and Mythic Wings in Sarah Orne Jewett and Toni Morrison: The Cultural Function of Narrative* (1992) and numerous articles on black women writers, African-American literature and culture, and Toni Morrison. Her work-in-progress is *Space for the Reader*, a study of Toni Morrison's narrative poetics and cultural politics.